The Love Puzzle

The Love Puzzle

Barbara Cartland

Thorndike Press • Chivers Press
Thorndike, Maine USA   Bath, England

This Large Print edition is published by Thorndike Press, USA and by Chivers Press, England.

Published in 2001 in the U.S. by arrangement with International Book Marketing Limited.

Published in 2001 in the U.K. by arrangement with Cartland Promotions.

U.S. Hardcover 0-7862-3279-X (Candlelight Series Edition)
U.K. Hardcover 0-7540-4521-8 (Chivers Large Print)
U.K. Softcover 0-7540-4522-6 (Camden Large Print)

The text of this Large Print edition is unabridged.
Other aspects of the book may vary from the original edition.

Set in 16 pt. Plantin by Al Chase.

Printed in the United States on permanent paper.

British Library Cataloguing-in-Publication Data available

Library of Congress Cataloging-in-Publication Data

Cartland, Barbara, 1902–
The love puzzle / Barbara Cartland.
p. cm.
ISBN: 0-7862-3279-X (lg. print : hc : alk. paper)
I. Title.
PR6005.A765 L6565 2001
823′.912—dc21 2001027098

AUTHOR'S NOTE

In this story the Duke is looking for the "Golden Fleece."

In Greek Legend, Jason and a band of heroes known as the Argonauts set out to find the Golden Fleece. This was the fleece of a ram which was sacrificed by Phrixus and hung in the Grove of Ares, guarded by a sleepless Dragon.

After many adventures and difficult obstacles had been overcome, Jason succeeded in carrying off the Golden Fleece.

"To seek the Golden Fleece" is now symbolic of man's effort to attempt the impossible.

chapter one

1872

"It is absolutely ridiculous!" Lady Branston stormed. "I cannot imagine anything the Duke will dislike more than having a stupid, unfledged young girl of eighteen at his party!"

"I see no reason at all why Katrina should be stupid," Lord Branston said somewhat pompously. "My brother-in-law was extremely intelligent and so was my sister."

His voice was firm as he added:

"The fact that they had very little money and lived abroad does not necessarily indicate a lack of brains."

The way he spoke told his wife that she had gone too far.

She could cajole and coax her husband into doing almost anything she wanted.

At the same time, he was very proud of his family.

Any slight on them always resulted in his being both irritated and obstinate.

"As it happens, I have already spoken to Lyndbrooke," Lord Branston went on, "and he said, of course, it would be perfectly all right to bring Katrina with us on Friday."

He paused before continuing:

"After all, his house is the size of an Army Barracks and there will be no difficulty about accommodating one more woman."

Lady Branston pressed her lips together.

She flounced across the room, her bustle swinging indignantly as she did so.

"Very well, Arthur," she said, "if that is your final decision, there is no point in my saying any more. But I hope you will be responsible for your niece."

She stopped speaking to look at him.

"You must make sure that everyone in the house-party is not furious at having a girl completely ignorant of everything in which they are interested thrust upon them. If you ask me, she will be a 'fish out of water.' "

With this parting shot she left and Lord Branston moved towards the fireplace with a sigh.

He should have known, he thought, that the idea of having Katrina in the house would upset Lucy.

'But what else,' he asked himself, 'could I have done about the child?'

When he learnt that his only sister and her husband had been killed together in a train accident in France, he had hurried across the Channel to where they had been living near Amiens.

It was a small house which was, however, he thought, comfortable and well decorated.

He found his niece stunned and bewildered to find that without any warning she was alone in the world.

"Papa and Mama," she told him, "were only going to Paris for two nights, as Papa wanted to see an Art Dealer about the picture he had just finished."

She was very pretty, Lord Branston thought, and despite her unhappiness, had an exceptional self-control.

He warmly and without any prevarication told her that in future she would live with him and he would look after her.

She had been so grateful and, he thought, very sensible.

He arranged for Katrina to follow him back to England properly chaperoned.

She had first to pack up all she wished to keep of her father's and mother's belongings.

It was only when he was alone that he wondered what Lucy would say about it.

Lord Branston had married for the second time when he was well over fifty, a very attractive, beautiful widow seventeen years younger than himself.

She had captivated and entranced him.

Also, as she came from a good family — he would not have considered her otherwise — it seemed eminently suitable that two widowed people should console each other.

It was only after their marriage that Lord Branston found that Lucy was not particularly unhappy that her first husband had departed this world.

In fact, if she were truthful, she was glad to be rid of him.

Lord Branston, on the other hand, had deeply mourned his wife.

He had loved her dearly, despite the fact that she had not given him children.

He had wanted a son.

He would also have liked a daughter whom he could have presented to the Social World, in which he had a definite place.

Lucy was only too willing to meet his distinguished friends and make her curtsy at Buckingham Palace.

She enjoyed every moment of playing hostess at his house in Brook Street, and his large, imposing mansion in the country.

She was well aware that the one thing her husband wanted was a son.

She was determined to give him one, but

it was important from her point of view that she should first establish herself as a beauty.

She also wished to be known as the "witty Lady Branston," as she complacently thought herself to be.

What she had not expected and had certainly never even envisaged was that she would fall in love.

The moment she saw the Duke of Lyndbrooke, she knew he was the man whom she should have married.

He was the embodiment of the Prince Charming she had dreamt of since she was a girl.

It did not matter that she was several years older than he was.

Nor that the Duke had declared his intention of never marrying however much he might be pressured by his relatives to do so.

If she could not marry him, Lucy knew that the next best thing was quite obvious.

It would only be a question of time before he succumbed to the wiles which during the years she had been a widow she had brought to a fine art.

Before she remarried she had not the means to decorate "the lily," as she thought of herself, with the right frame for her beauty.

Lord Branston, however, was exceedingly

generous when it came to clothes and jewels.

When she was sparkling like a Christmas tree, Lucy was sure that no man, let alone the Duke, would be able to resist her.

At the same time, she was up against a considerable amount of rivalry.

The Social World — headed by the Prince of Wales — enjoyed itself despite the gloom emanating from Windsor Castle.

There was not a woman in it who did not think it would be a "feather in her cap" if the Duke so much as noticed her.

Lucy was confident of her own attractions.

What she did not want was a distraction in the shape of a young girl whom she would have to chaperon.

A girl who would obviously cling to her like, she thought, a piece of poison ivy.

When she reached her bedroom, Lucy stamped her foot and allowed her anger to contort her lovely face.

Then she caught sight of herself in the mirror.

She knew that to indulge such emotions would undoubtedly carve lines on her delicate skin.

With a superhuman effort she forced herself to sit down calmly at her dressing-table.

She contemplated her own reflection in the mirror.

She was certainly very alluring with her hair slightly touched up — although no one was aware of it — to inflect the deep gold of the sun before it sinks behind the horizon.

Her eyes were the blue of the Mediterranean.

Her lips, which many men had told her invited their kisses, were quite perfect in shape.

"Why should I worry when I look like this?" Lucy asked herself.

Yet she thought it would be an encumbrance to have with her a young girl who was a *débutante*.

The prospect infuriated her so that she wanted to scream.

It was not that the tiresome child would compete in any way.

It was just that she wished to be the only star in the firmament, and that the Duke, and everybody else for that matter, should think that she was alone in her glory.

Lord Branston had returned to Branston House and told her that Katrina would be arriving in three or four days' time.

She had not at first understood that he intended the girl to remain with them until she was married.

"Would it not be best, Arthur dear," she said, "if your niece has a Governess or some suitable companion to retire with her to the country until the Season is over? After all, she is in deep mourning and cannot even attend a tea-party, let alone anything gayer."

"That is where you are wrong," Lord Branston had replied.

Lucy looked at him enquiringly, and he explained:

"Katrina told me that neither her father nor my sister approved of mourning. In fact, as the girl put it, they did not believe in death!"

"What on earth did she mean by that?" Lucy asked, her voice rising.

"As you know, my sister and her husband lived in India when they were first married, and apparently they became interested in Buddhism. They therefore believed that nobody dies, but lives on eternally."

"I have never heard such nonsense in the whole of my life!" Lucy said sharply. "How can people accept anything so foolish, so utterly unrealistic? You have seen dead bodies, and so have I! And very dead they are before they are put into their coffins and lowered down into the ground!"

Lord Branston sighed before he said:

"I think quite a lot of people would disagree with you, and, in fact, I have often thought it reasonable and just that all our struggling to improve ourselves in this life should not be lost forever."

"I do not know what you are talking about," Lucy said firmly, "but I have no intention of listening any further to such rubbish!"

"Whether you listen or not," Lord Branston said, "while Katrina is extremely unhappy at losing her parents, she is quite certain that they are together and watching over her, and she has no intention of wearing black."

He paused and then continued:

"She will therefore attend the parties we give and those we go to as if nothing untoward has occurred."

"Well, I think it is extraordinary and extremely unnatural that a young girl, if she had any love for her mother and father, should not be crying her eyes out."

"I have just explained to you, Lucy," Lord Branston said with a note of irritability in his voice, "that she does not believe they are dead."

"As far as I am concerned, she should be locked up in a Lunatic Asylum!" Lucy retorted.

Then as she glanced at her husband's face she realised she had made a mistake.

In the soft, gentle voice that she knew he found irresistible she said:

"I am sorry, dearest Arthur, that you have lost your sister. I know how fond you were of her, even though she lived abroad, and, of course, we must do our best for poor orphaned Katrina."

"That is what I wanted you to say," Lord Branston said heavily, patting his wife's shoulder, "and I shall look to you, my dear, to dress her as befits my niece and make sure she is a social success."

It was then that it flashed through Lucy's mind that the sooner she could get the girl up the aisle, the better.

By the time Katrina arrived in London, she had already decided what gowns she would buy for her and from which shops she would obtain them.

What she had not expected, however, was that Katrina in her own way would be a beauty.

The moment she walked into the house Lucy had a shock.

Although she was unaware of it, for a moment her own lovely face looked quite ugly.

Katrina was actually so different from what she had expected.

Lucy knew that her husband's sister, whom she had never seen, was considered to be very pretty.

Her husband with whom she had fallen madly in love was a handsome man.

What she had thought ridiculous was that Elizabeth could have shone in the Social World which she herself thought so important.

Instead, she had married a man who had neither wealth nor position simply because she fell in love.

According to Lord Branston, there had been quite a number of distinguished young aristocrats ready to dance attendance on his sister from the moment she left the School-Room.

Through some oversight on the part of their parents, Michael Darley had come to their house in the country.

He had been asked as an extra man for a dinner-party Elizabeth's parents were giving before the Hunt Ball.

He had been staying with a raffish Peer who had taken a liking to him.

He was an excellent rider and on his horses won all the local Steeple-Chases and the Point-to-Points.

As a great concession, for she was not yet a *débutante,* Elizabeth had been allowed to come down to dinner.

Some of her mother and father's guests had suggested she go on to the Hunt Ball.

Wearing a pretty but simple gown with no jewellery, she had looked very different from the other tiaraed ladies.

Bedecked in huge crinolines which made it difficult for them to sit down, they were sensational.

Elizabeth had been a natural daisy amongst a profusion of exotic orchids.

Michael Darley had lost his heart and captured hers.

They waited six months, during which time Michael Darley became almost a permanent guest in his friend's house.

For the first time in her life Elizabeth was deceitful.

She made arrangements to ride alone so that she could meet Michael in the woods.

They also met at several local parties.

It was an absolute bomb-shell to her father and mother when they announced that they wished to become engaged.

Lord and Lady Branston pleaded with their daughter almost on their knees to have a Season in London as had been planned.

Surely, they enquired, she wanted to make her curtsy to the Queen before she even thought of marriage with Darley or any other man.

But it was to no avail.

Elizabeth was in love, head over heels in love.

Her parents were forced to realise that any opposition was hopeless, and eventually consented to their engagement.

Almost before it was in the newspapers Michael and Elizabeth were pressing for a date on which they could be married.

Because it would obviously be a waste of time to argue with them, Lord and Lady Branston finally capitulated.

It was difficult to imagine any two people could be more happy.

They had very little money, living mostly on a small allowance that Elizabeth received from her father.

Nothing mattered because they were together.

They travelled all over the world cheaply, often in very uncomfortable conditions, and loved every moment of it.

When Michael discovered he had a talent for painting, they settled in France, where there was more appreciation of art than in England.

That was not to say that he made very much money from his paintings.

He was paid nothing for the kind of pictures he preferred painting.

He liked to paint in the style of the men

who called themselves "Impressionists."

It did not worry him that they were laughed at and decried by every critic who saw their work.

Michael, however, could also paint what he called "pot boilers."

These sold well because they were pretty and imaginative.

He made enough money for a few small luxuries.

He ensured that Elizabeth had the clothes which made her look as beautiful as she had been when he first saw her.

They were poor, of course they were poor, but only as regards money.

Their house was filled with laughter, intelligent conversation, and with new ideas which attracted to them unusual people.

Besides, they saved painstakingly to enable them to visit every year some part of the world they had not already seen.

Katrina was taken to Greece when she was only five.

Two years later she visited Turkey with them, and the year after that Egypt.

There the food was often bad and their lodgings uncomfortable.

Yet they saw sights which other people spent hundreds of pounds on their journeys to see and missed.

They would return home with paintings that Michael Darley could sell very easily because they were what he called "pretty-pretty."

Yet Katrina had loved them.

When she arrived in London she brought few clothes even though her trunks contained her own as well as her mother's things.

But every picture, every sketch, everything she could collect of her father's came with her.

They had been packed carefully in trunks she had bought cheaply in the Market.

"I do not know what you are going to do with all this rubbish!" Lucy had said scornfully when she saw what the trunks contained.

"Uncle Arthur said I could bring with me everything I wanted to keep that belonged to Mama and Papa," Katrina answered.

"You cannot get into your bedroom with all that cluttering up the place," Lucy replied. "Take out only what is absolutely necessary and tell the servants to put the trunks up in the attic. You can always look at them there, if you have nothing better to do."

Katrina did not answer — she did not expect her aunt to understand.

She had sensed even before Lucy talked to her that she was antagonistic, and resentful that she had come to live with them.

'I must leave if I can find somewhere else,' she thought a little helplessly.

But for the moment, at any rate, she knew she must be as self-effacing as possible.

She hoped that her Aunt Lucy did not really dislike her as much as she appeared to.

It was a forlorn hope.

When she was alone at night she would talk to her mother and tell her how difficult it was.

"I am doing my best, Mama," she would say in the darkness, "but I can feel Aunt Lucy's hatred of me coming towards me in waves. Although I know you would . . . expect me to behave as you and Papa would do . . . it is very . . . very difficult!"

She was quite certain her mother could hear what she was saying and understand.

She always felt that her father and mother were very close to her and she was not alone.

It was only this, she told herself, which made the first few days in London tolerable.

She was forced to face the truth that her life had changed completely.

Never again would she know the happiness, the joy and delight of being with two people who loved each other and her so completely.

'Uncle Arthur is kind, very kind in his own way,' she thought, 'but there is no love in this grand, rather frightening house.'

She had sensed that everything in it was for show.

The big Drawing-Room, with its stiff expensively brocaded furniture and its hothouse flowers arranged methodically in crystal vases, was so unlike the easy comfort of the small Sitting-Room of their house in France.

Then there were the flowers which she had picked from the garden or the fields.

She had arranged them with loving care, so that her father would often exclaim when he saw them:

"I must paint those, they are perfect and just what some old lady will want to remind her of her first love — an ardent young man."

He had laughed as he said this because it sounded so ridiculous, and Katrina had laughed too.

Then she would carry the flowers carefully into the small room at the back of the house.

It had a north light and her father called it his "Studio."

He would paint the flowers, telling her it would make a contribution to the housekeeping money, and she was a clever girl.

She would not have been human if she had not been pleased with the gowns her aunt bought for her.

Even though she knew Aunt Lucy grudged the trouble and expense.

The waves of hatred when she was dressed seemed almost to strike her with their intensity.

"I cannot think why you do not look like other *débutantes,*" Lucy asked once.

Katrina, looking in her mirror, could understand her aunt's exasperation.

She did look different.

She could see it herself when she went to her first evening party, at which there were several *débutantes,* all dressed carefully in white.

They either sat tongue-tied and shy when anyone approached them, or else giggled amongst themselves.

Because Katrina had gone everywhere with her father and mother, she had met so many different people of different nationalities.

After talking with many diverse personalities, she was not in the least shy.

She had learnt from her father to find

almost everybody she met interesting, and in different ways.

"Everybody has something about them which makes their heart beat faster when they think about it," Michael Darley had said.

He paused before he went on:

"What you have to do is to draw it out of them, mesmerise them, if you like, into telling you what they feel and what they think. That is what makes every man and woman, unless they are complete 'clots,' interesting individuals."

"I know what you are saying, Papa," Katrina had answered, "but it is difficult."

"Of course it is difficult," her father had answered, "but think of yourself as one of the Archaeologists we saw in Egypt looking for treasure that has been made in the tombs."

He threw out his hand as he continued:

"Or the Curators in Greece who fight a constant battle with the vandals who would damage or destroy the wonders of the past."

He winked at Katrina before he ended:

"How do you know that you will not find something just as exciting and just as valuable simply by delving into the heart and soul of someone who outwardly looks just like a fat toad?"

Katrina had laughed, and after that she had often said to her father:

"What do you think I discovered today?"

She would then tell him how she had met a woman who had seemed dull and uninteresting.

"Yet, do you know, Papa, for years she has been collecting rare plants and herbs which she has pressed and kept for her own enjoyment, too shy to show them to anybody else."

She learned also of a politician who was very courageous in the Chamber of Deputies, but was secretly afraid of ghosts.

There was a trader in cattle her mother had talked to in the Market who always called to see her every time he came to Amiens.

He bred cats, the soft blue Persians, which few people had seen in the part of the country where he lived.

It certainly fascinated Katrina to learn about people.

It was less interesting when she could no longer relate to her father her discoveries or discuss them with him.

"As far as Aunt Lucy is concerned," she told him a few nights after she had arrived in London, "she seems to be encompassed by a kind of . . . armour and as she hates . . . me

. . . it is impossible for me to get . . . near her."

She knew her father would understand.

There was no need to explain to him that her aunt disliked her not only as a person, but mostly because of her appearance.

Looking in her mirror, Katrina saw her face was very young, perhaps in some ways childlike.

At the same time, she had what her father had called a "spiritual look."

It was something he had tried to put down on canvas but always felt he had failed.

"How can any man paint what he feels rather than sees," he asked angrily.

"That is what the Impressionists try to do," Katrina answered.

"Then I am a bad Impressionist!" he said. "Nevertheless, we will try again another day, but it is difficult, very difficult where you are concerned, my dearest."

"I think your picture is rather good, Papa."

"Not good enough," Michael had said. "You are beautiful, but it is a beauty that comes from inside, like a Chinese drawing which always has an inner meaning which is as difficult to capture as a 'will-o'-the-wisp' or a shooting-star."

Katrina had laughed.

"Now you are making me feel important!"

Her father put his arm round her.

"You are very, very important to me," he said, "and one day, my darling, you will be very important to the man who loves you, if he is intelligent enough to realise that, like your mother, you are unique and very different from other women."

"Were you aware of that when you first met Mama?"

Her father had smiled.

"The moment I saw her on the other side of the Dining-Room table I felt as if my heart left my body. She was so lovely, but it was much more than that."

He drew in his breath:

"It was the meeting of two people who have been together for eternity and could never really be separated in this world or any other."

'That is what I want to find some day,' Katrina thought.

She had the discouraging feeling that it was something she would never find amongst the people her Aunt Lucy entertained.

Then she told herself she was judging too quickly.

Her mother would say she must take

things slowly and try to understand other people's points of view.

"You see, darling," she had explained, "we are put into this world to grow spiritually and to progress in the development of our personalities. The further we go, the more we realise there is for us to understand and learn."

She smiled as she went on:

"It is all very thrilling and exciting, like the sound of beautiful music which becomes more and more meaningful the more often you hear it."

She knew her daughter was listening as she said quietly:

"But not everybody develops in the same way, and therefore it is no use being impatient with those who are less proficient than ourselves."

She sighed and continued:

"Perhaps they are proficient in a way in which we are not clever enough to understand. But we must try — try very hard — and that is where you will not only help people, but influence them."

Katrina had been very young when her mother had said this to her, but she had always remembered it.

She told herself now that she was being far too impatient and far too censorious.

She had the feeling that she would never get to know Aunt Lucy in the right way.

That she would just have to admit failure.

Her aunt had certainly objected strongly to her being invited to stay with the Duke of Lyndbrooke.

This had made everything worse than it was already.

Katrina learned that it was a party that had been arranged some time ago.

Her Aunt Lucy had obviously been looking forward to it eagerly.

She had, in fact, ordered a number of gowns for herself at the same time as she was buying Katrina's.

Katrina had heard her say to the *Vendeuse* who had attended to her and whom she apparently knew very well:

"You understand that I want to wear these at Lynd when we are staying with the Duke, so they must be ready for next Thursday."

"You are going to Lynd, M'Lady? That's very exciting!"

"I am sure it will be," Katrina heard her aunt reply complacently, "and this is a very special occasion, so you will understand that I want to look my best."

"Yes, of course, M'Lady! I think I could interest you in a new model which has just arrived and which is exactly the colour of Your Ladyship's eyes."

Aunt Lucy had bought two blue gowns as well as a number of others.

Katrina could not help thinking she would have to stay at least a month to wear them all.

They were certainly very beautiful with their bustles, which in the last four years had completely supplanted the crinoline.

They were of exquisite materials which she knew came from France.

Katrina was delighted with her own gowns.

Especially those which were plainer and not so frilled and exaggerated as her aunt's.

Hers put her in mind of the Greek statues she had seen in Athens.

They had the exquisite drapery which had survived in stone for centuries and which neither the vandals nor the sun or rain had damaged or ruined.

Only when she overheard the angry protests at her being included in the party invited to Lynd did she realise how much the visit meant to her aunt.

She had the distinct feeling that this had something to do with the Duke.

Her aunt right up to the last moment tried to persuade Lord Branston that Katrina should be left at home.

"Do you realise," she heard her aunt say, "that the Duke has asked all his closest friends to this party? They are about his age and will have nothing in common, nothing at all, with Katrina!"

Her husband had not answered for the simple reason that he had heard this before.

Besides, like all older men who dislike being thwarted, he was determined to have his own way.

"I am taking Katrina with us to Lynd," he said firmly and finally. "As I told you, I spoke to Lyndbrooke about it and I have no doubt that by this time he has asked some young man who is nearer her age than yours."

Katrina thought that this was, in a way, an insult to her aunt.

She was not surprised, therefore, that her Aunt Lucy said when they were alone:

"You are a very lucky girl to be going to Lynd, and I hope you appreciate the fact and do not make a nuisance of yourself."

"I shall try not to, Aunt Lucy," Katrina said.

"Then keep out of the Duke's way and do not impose yourself on his friends."

"I will try not to do that, Aunt Lucy."

"Your uncle has it in his head that you

cannot stay here alone while we go away, even though I suggested half-a-dozen relations who would be only too delighted to come and chaperon you."

The note of irritation in her voice was very obvious, and Katrina thought it wiser to say nothing.

"No one can say," her aunt went on, "that I have not done my best for you. There is no *débutante* in the whole of London who has better clothes, and if you are a failure, it will be no use blaming me."

"I am very grateful for the lovely gowns, Aunt Lucy," Katrina replied, "and if it upsets you, I am quite content to stay here."

"That is what you should do!" Lucy snapped. "But your uncle has made up his mind, and nothing short of an earthquake will change it!"

She looked at her niece, then she said:

"As I have said, I have done my best. If you do not look as a *débutante* should, the only hope for you is to try to behave like one!"

She flashed a look of hatred from her blue eyes at Katrina.

Then she went from the room, slamming the door behind her.

Katrina gave a little sigh.

'It is hopeless,' she thought. 'How can I

change my looks just to suit Aunt Lucy?'

She got up from the chair in which she had been sitting and looked at herself in the large mirror over the mantelshelf.

It reflected the Sevres vases and a large Ormulu clock which had come from France.

Between them she could see herself.

Her large eyes, which were the soft grey of a pigeon's breast, seemed to dominate her small, heart-shaped face.

Her hair was so pale that her father had said:

"If you had pink eyes, you would have been an albino, and that would have been disastrous!"

"Perhaps I could dye it, Papa!" she suggested jokingly.

Her father had given a cry of horror.

"Do not dare touch it," he said. "It is lovely, like the first pale fingers of the dawn. Only an artist could have thought of giving you a skin that is as white as the first snowdrops and lips that are the soft pink of a musk rose."

"Now you are being poetical, Papa!" Katrina laughed.

"I suppose, as your mother and I love each other so much, that it was inevitable we should produce something so beautiful, although it is certainly not the conventional beauty which most people admire."

As he spoke he looked across the room at his easel.

On it was a canvas depicting a very florid woman with golden hair and blue eyes silhouetted against blue velvet curtains.

It was the conventional type of picture her father hated.

But it had been commissioned by the Dutch Counsel and portrayed his wife.

It would, as Katrina knew, be very much admired when it was hung in his rather ostentatious house.

Looking back now, Katrina thought perhaps it was a pity she did not look more like that, then perhaps Aunt Lucy would be pleased with her.

She remembered then that her Aunt Lucy had all the attributes of beauty which her father despised: golden hair, blue eyes, and pink-and-white complexion.

"It is too obvious, too ordinary!" he had stormed as he painted the Mayor's daughter. "It makes me want to go out and pick up some woman from the gutter and see if I can find her soul!"

"Instead of which," Katrina's mother remarked, "the money you will get for that picture, darling, will afford us a delicious and very expensive dinner, and the rest of it will go into our fund at the bank to pay for our holiday next year. Have you decided where we shall go?"

"I thought we might fly to the moon," Michael Darley answered, "or perhaps if you think that would be too cold, we might try Morocco."

The way he spoke made both his wife and daughter give a cry of delight.

"Can we really go there?"

"I have a wild desire to see you both silhouetted against the Atlas Mountains," he replied.

Then they were both kissing him because it was so exciting.

'Now, I suppose,' Katrina said to herself wistfully, 'I shall never see the Atlas Mountains.'

Then, as she glanced again at her reflection, she heard her father say almost as if he stood beside her:

"One day the man you love will take you there."

chapter two

The Duke of Lyndbrooke looked around the Drawing-Room of Devonshire House and thought he would enjoy the party.

Mr. Disraeli was there and the Earl of Kimberley, Secretary of State for Foreign Affairs.

There were several other Statesmen to whom he enjoyed talking, besides the most beautiful women in London.

He was just contemplating which of the beauties should engage his attention, when the Butler announced:

"The Earl and Countess of Calverton, Your Grace!"

If the Duke had not been so self-controlled, he would have been startled.

As it was, he was still for a moment.

Then, very slowly, he turned his head to look at the new arrivals coming through the ornate doorway.

He was not mistaken.

Anastasia was being greeted by the Duchess of Devonshire, and behind her was the stout, burly figure of her husband, the Earl.

For a moment the Duke was swept back into the past when he had first met Anastasia.

He had been in the wilds of Malaya, tiger-hunting.

When he came down to Singapore, he met her at the first party to which he was invited.

He had thought that she herself looked like a tigress.

Russian, she had just been bereaved, he was told, her husband, a tea-planter, having died of the fever that was so prevalent in certain parts of the country.

As a widow, she was certainly not mourning the deceased.

By the end of the evening, as she concentrated her strange green eyes on him, the Duke had been fascinated by her.

Not that he had been a Duke in those days, but Tristram Brooke, exploring the world.

His father, who was a first cousin of the Sixth Duke of Lyndbrooke, was not rich and could afford to give him only a small allowance.

He had spent two years in the family Regiment, but found it too restricting.

Much to his parents' displeasure, he had bought himself out and decided to go East.

"It is a waste of your time and my money!" his father had thundered at him.

"I promise you, Father, I will be as economical as possible, but if I do not see the world now, I may never have another chance."

They both knew he meant that he might be married.

He would be tied down and restricted by a wife and family and would undoubtedly have to find some regular means of providing for them.

As it was, if he was living in extreme discomfort and even had to go without food, he had only himself to think about.

He also, which he could not explain to his father, had an urgent desire to see some of the sights which even to read about them gave him a strange feeling.

In fact, they excited his mind and invigorated his heart.

It was not something that he could put into words, and yet he knew that these were sensations and desires he could not ignore.

Whatever anyone else said, he must satisfy his curiosity about them.

He spent a short time in India, and knew when he left it, it was a place to which he would return.

Malaya was next on his programme — not that he had one written on paper but only in his mind — and he was not disappointed.

The beauty of Malaya, the flowers, even the tigers that stalked the forest and, incidentally, killed a number of labourers, entranced him.

The whole scene was so different from anything he had encountered before.

Singapore was also fascinating, with its Chinese population, the beauty of its seafront, and with what he realised were the immense possibilities of development.

Then once he had met Anastasia it was difficult to think of anything else.

He had never met or imagined any woman could be like her.

She entwined herself round him like the clinging vegetation which smothered the trees in the forest.

He thought it would be impossible for him to escape from her.

He had fallen in love as only a young man, full of ideals, who had never been disillusioned, could be in love.

He thought that Anastasia loved him in return.

But he learnt he had not enough to offer, and when he asked her to marry him, she merely laughed at him.

"On what would we live, *Mon Cher?*" she enquired.

She spoke French when he was making love to her because in Russia the aristocrats, from the Tsar downwards, always spoke French.

Although it was doubtful if Anastasia had ever moved in Russian Court Circles, she was determined to behave as if she had.

She called herself Countess, though it was unlikely that she was one.

But as there were nearly a million Countesses in Russia, it was impossible for anyone to check the authenticity of her claim.

"Marry me, Anastasia! We will be very happy together. I will work so that I can buy you everything you want," Tristram Brooke had said passionately.

"Do you really think we would be happy living in a cottage, counting every penny, not being able to afford to go to London, to entertain or be entertained?" Anastasia asked.

She threw up her hands as if to fend him off before she said:

"*Non, Non, Mon Brave,* that is not what I want of life. I want security and that means a great deal of money. I want also a position — a social position . . . of great importance."

Tristram Brooke had been silent.

He had nothing to offer her except, when his father died, an ancient Manor house in the country.

If they visited London, they would certainly never be able to afford to entertain the Social World which meant so much to Anastasia.

He spent a month with her in Singapore, making love to her.

He found that she had a power to arouse a man to the heights of fiery desire without ever seeming to be satisfied herself.

When she left him, he had returned to India, where, after staying on the way in Ceylon, he travelled very widely.

Not that he travelled in comfort, but in the cheapest carriages on the trains or on the roads in carts overcrowded with natives.

It had all been a great experience.

Yet the beauty of the women's *saris,* the flowers they wore in their hair, and the pungent scent of the perfumes in the Bazaar often reminded him too poignantly of Anastasia.

During the course of his travels there had inevitably been other women.

He was far too attractive.

Besides, he belonged to a very distinguished family, so he was invited to dine by the Viceroy and the Governor as well as the

Regiments in every Province he visited.

From India he had continued his travels homewards, not hurrying, but savouring all the places he wanted to see.

He was actually in Babylon when he read a month-old English newspaper which had been left there by a Commercial Traveller.

He learnt that the present Duke of Lyndbrooke was dead, and so was his father.

He could hardly credit what he was reading.

When he had left England, the Duke's only son, a robust young man, was very much alive.

He had, however, been killed, Tristram Brooke was informed, by a bad fall out hunting after he himself had reached Malaya.

The next heir to the title was his father, and now he, too, was dead.

The newspaper said that the Trustees and Solicitors of the estate were "searching for Tristram Brooke, who was believed to be travelling in foreign parts."

He went home as quickly as he could, but it was a month before he arrived in England.

Then he learnt that he was not only the Seventh Duke of Lyndbrooke, but also one of the wealthiest men in the country.

His ancestral home, which was considered to be Adam's masterpiece, was one of the finest ever built.

He also owned numerous estates in other parts of the country.

Because he had faced life the hard way, the new Duke was not overcome or even deeply elated by the manner in which he was treated by everybody he met.

It was very different from his reception in the past.

When he had been a handsome young man with no prospects, ambitious mothers had hurried their daughters away the moment he appeared.

Married women condescended to him, attracted by his masculinity but aware that his pockets were empty.

Now everything was different.

He was fawned on, pursued, relentlessly stalked by women as if he were a stag.

There was no doubt he enjoyed himself.

At the same time, Anastasia had taught him a lesson where women were concerned which he knew he could never forget.

To a woman, money and position meant more than love.

He told himself he would never give his heart to a woman again, knowing it had little value apart from the coronet he wore.

Once in a mood, which he despised as

being sentimental, he told himself that Anastasia had killed his dreams.

Now he was prepared to face the world on its own terms.

It was certainly a very pleasant world.

In the last five years since he had become the Duke he had found it comfortable to have innumerable servants to wait on him.

To know that in his own domain his word was law.

He could watch his horses gallop first past the winning-post in Classic races, aware that his stables were filled with the finest horseflesh obtainable.

There was a great deal to organise.

He felt sometimes as if he were a Colonel in command of a very large and very smart Regiment which nevertheless had to be kept up to scratch.

He was offered a number of positions at Court.

Because he was so good-looking, the Queen, although shrouded in black crêpe and weeping incessantly for her beloved Albert, wanted him continually in attendance.

He managed to avoid being caught in that snare.

He told the Prime Minister not to pressure him into taking on duties which would encroach on his freedom:

"If I am pushed too hard, Prime Minister, I shall give up everything and go abroad. There are still many parts of the world I am longing to see, and I can now do it in a great deal more comfort than I did before."

The Prime Minister smiled.

"I wonder if, in fact, you will find it so satisfactory when you are cushioned from harsh reality."

There was no answer to this, the Duke recognised.

When he journeyed to his Villa in the South of France, he had a sudden longing for the empty barrenness of the desert on the other side of the Mediterranean.

For the hot sun, for the camels, and the smell of the land which was as uncivilised as the people who inhabited it.

"Sooner or later, I must get away," he told himself.

Yet there was always some "Fair Charmer" to pull him back to London, to England, and to Lynd.

It was Lynd which made him feel that all the pomp and circumstance which he had laughed at cynically was worthwhile.

It was so beautiful, with its Ionic Columns on the porticoed front.

The Picture Gallery contained treasures that had been collected by the family since the first Brooke had been created a Knight after the Battle of Agincourt.

Sometimes when he was alone, which was not very often, the Duke would walk around the house.

He felt he wanted to touch every picture, every statue, every book, and every case to make sure they were real.

He was still afraid they were just part of his imagination.

"Mine! Mine!" he would say to himself.

Then he remembered he was only a trustee of the house and its treasures for his lifetime, and they belonged to those who would come after him.

To his son, if he had one, or to another cousin, as he had been himself, and there were plenty of them.

There were also plenty of women to tell him that he was exactly the right person to be the Duke of Lyndbrooke.

"You are such a perfect lover," a very beautiful lady had murmured in his ear last night. "It seems somehow unfair you should also be so rich and a Duke!"

"I wonder if you would appreciate me so much if I were only the first," the Duke had said mockingly.

"You know I love you for yourself as a man," she answered passionately.

He remembered that was what Anastasia had said, until he had asked her to marry him and she had laughed.

Now, when he told himself she was no longer of any interest to him, she had appeared.

He had, of course, learnt that soon after she had left him in Singapore, she had married the Earl of Calverton.

He thought scornfully that she had certainly found her rich man who also had the rank she craved.

When he heard the news, he had for several weeks walked about with a stormy expression in his eyes and a cruel twist to his lips.

Then, inevitably, he had been charmed out of what he described to himself as a "fit of the sullens" by somebody who was the very opposite of Anastasia.

She was soft, gentle, very sweet, and looked at him adoringly.

She told him a thousand times that if she were not already married, she would beg him on her knees to marry her.

He was glad the situation did not arise.

At the same time, he found her a comfort physically.

When he left her, he was once more finding the world an intriguing place and was just as curious about it as he had been before.

Now, as he watched Anastasia greet her host and two other people she knew, he thought the years since they had met had been kind to her.

She was now, in fact, even more exotically beautiful than he remembered.

It might be, he thought cynically, the gown she wore, which she certainly could not have afforded as his wife.

Her jewels, which he suspected were family ones, were outstanding.

Her tiara of emeralds and diamonds and the necklace which matched it reflecting the green of her eyes.

Then she turned to look at him.

He was aware that while he had not been expecting to see her, she had known that he would be a guest at that night's dinner-party.

She moved towards him, not hurrying, but with a sinuous grace which he remembered.

It brought into play every muscle in her lissom body.

Now her hand was in his and as she looked up at him she said very softly:

"You are still very handsome, *Mon Cher!*"

He laughed.

It was so like Anastasia to say the unexpected, and he replied:

"Let me return the compliment. You are even lovelier than when I last saw you!"

"That is what I wanted you to think," she said very softly, "and we must talk together. I have so much to tell you."

"No, Anastasia!" the Duke wanted to say.

But even as his lips moved, Anastasia glided away from him and he found himself face to face with the Earl.

"How are you, Lyndbrooke?" he asked in his thick, ageing voice. "I heard a great deal about you from my wife, and your horse, I regret to say, beat mine last week at Epsom."

"I remember that," the Duke replied, "but I did not see you there."

"No, we have been in Paris," the Earl explained. "I had a message to convey from Her Majesty to our Ambassador, and, needless to say, my wife could not be dragged home without first providing herself with enough new gowns to dress the whole chorus at Drury Lane!"

The Duke laughed.

He had not met the Earl before, and he rather liked him.

The Earl was older than he had expected, but he was certain that would not trouble Anastasia.

He found this was true when the lady sitting next to him at dinner said:

"I see my *bête noir* is here, which always spoils a party for me."

"And who is that?" the Duke asked, because it was expected of him.

"The Countess of Calverton," she replied. "I detest her, mostly because men find her irresistible, and by all accounts she feels the same about them!"

The words were spiteful and the speaker's eyes were hard.

Looking at Anastasia on the other side of the table, he could understand.

He watched her flirting with the men on either side of her at the long table and obviously holding them enthralled.

Later, after dinner, when some of the guests wandered into the garden at the back of the house, Anastasia joined the Duke.

He had been talking to the Prime Minister.

Then — he was not certain how she managed it — he found himself walking alone with her over the lawn under the shadow of the trees.

The stars were out and the garden was discreetly lit.

It was possible to see her green eyes looking up at him as she said softly:

"When am I going to see you? Hugo always goes to his Club in the afternoon."

"No, Anastasia!"

"What do you mean, no?" she enquired. "I have a great deal to talk to you about, and, after all, you are a very old — friend."

There was just a slight hesitation before the last word, which gave it a piquant meaning.

"I said 'No' and I mean 'No'!" the Duke said firmly. "You tortured me enough, Anastasia, but now I have learnt to live without you and I have no intention of going back on the rack!"

Anastasia laughed, and it was the sound of a woman who was very sure of herself.

Then she said in a different tone:

"Oh, *Mon Brave,* how could I have been so foolish as not to marry you when you asked me to do so? But how could I have known, how could I have guessed, that you would become who you are?"

She gave a deep sigh.

"I would have made you a very commendable Duchess."

"Instead of which you are a very commendable Countess!" the Duke replied. "So let us forget the past and go our separate ways, as you intended to do when you left me."

"There has never been another man like you!" Anastasia averred.

"And there have been a great many against whom to compare me!"

"Of course!" Anastasia admitted.

He had to laugh because it was so like her not to prevaricate.

They had now reached the end of the lawn and, turning round, were moving slowly back towards the house.

"You will come and see me to-morrow?"

"It is impossible, even if I wished to do so," the Duke replied. "I am going to Lynd, where I shall be entertaining a party."

"Is the house as beautiful as I have always heard it is?"

"Magnificent!" the Duke replied.

He wanted to extol the wonders of Lynd just to hurt her, then as she was silent he said firmly:

"Whatever you are thinking, Anastasia, the answer is 'No!' 'Once bitten, twice shy!' is a motto I have every intention of remembering! And now, having got what you wanted, you should make an effort to behave yourself."

"Who is likely to make me do that except you, my dearest?" Anastasia asked. "I adored you because you were so dominating, so masterful, so very different from other men, who always grovelled at my feet."

What she was saying he knew was true.

When he was jealous he had often been very rough with her, shaking her when she flirted with other men and threatening to beat her if she persisted.

He knew there was something wild and Russian in her.

It amused him to think now of how she had paid the penalty for her sins.

They stopped in the light from the windows and the Duke said:

"Good-night, Anastasia, and good-bye! It has been pleasant meeting you again, but remember, the answer is 'No.' "

"Can you be so certain of that?" she asked.

He knew she was laughing at him.

He went back into the Drawing-Room and sat down beside the Chancellor of the Exchequer to talk to him of the coming Budget.

They were soon interrupted, and the Duke realised for the first time that Lady Branston had been in the party at dinner.

He had not noticed her before because it had been impossible for him to think of anybody but Anastasia.

Now, because Lady Branston was very

beautiful and he knew all too clearly that she was attracted by him, he turned to her as if for relief from his thoughts.

"I am so looking forward to coming to Lynd to-morrow," she said in a beguiling fashion which he thought was attractive.

She was certainly a complete contrast from Anastasia.

Her gold hair and blue eyes had a loveliness that was very English and, he thought, straight-forward and not in the least exotic.

"I am looking forward to showing you my house and my treasures," the Duke replied.

"That will be very exciting!" Lady Branston said. "And because it all belongs to you, it will, I know, seem like a fairy-tale."

There was no mistaking that the smile she gave him was very inviting.

"I want you to enjoy yourself," the Duke said, "and if you tell me what you wish to do, we will do it together."

He was flirting with her in a manner which reciprocated her attitude towards him.

He was quite certain that at the first possible opportunity she would be in his arms.

He had been aware of what Lady Branston felt about him as soon as they met, and yet she had been clever enough not to seem blatant.

He might even have thought, had he not been so cynical, that he was pursuing her rather than the reverse.

At the moment, the Duke was willing to be pursued.

He was well aware that there were few, if any, women in the Social World in which he moved who were as beautiful as Lady Branston or as witty.

He knew no one would think it in the least wrong if he made love to her, as long as they were discreet about it.

He had no knowledge of Lord Branston's feelings in the matter.

But Lady Branston had already insinuated very cleverly on several occasions when they had talked together that her husband was old and did not understand her.

This meant, the Duke knew, that he did not make love to her as often as she wished.

There was, therefore, a place in her life for a lover.

He had long ago given up thinking, or expecting, that women should be faithful to their husbands.

When he was young, he had imagined that all "nice" women were like his mother.

Devoted and in a way dedicated to the men they married.

He had found when he was in India that the English women in the hill-stations had little thought for their husbands sweating it out on the plains.

In other countries, too, there were always attractive ladies who would creep into his room by night.

Although if they were alone, they would beg him to come to theirs.

In London it seemed too easy, as the husbands of beautiful women almost automatically went to their Clubs in the afternoon.

They stayed there until it was time to go home and dress for dinner.

At first the Duke had told himself it was too much trouble to make love to a pretty woman when he would rather be out riding.

Or, what he also enjoyed, listening to the political debates in the House of Lords.

Then he was beguiled by the invitation in a pair of lovely eyes and lips that waited eagerly for his.

Hands were clasped round his neck almost before he knew their Christian names.

He would not have been a man, let alone an extremely virile one, if he had not succumbed.

It was, he supposed, the fashion, and it

admittedly gave him a great deal of pleasure.

It was all part and parcel of his new position, his title, his houses, his horses, his pictures.

As one *affaire de coeur* ended, another began.

He gave it all his attention while in the lady's company.

It did not concern him greatly at other times.

Only occasionally, when he was looking at an exquisite view, or hearing music which seemed to echo within his heart, did he ask himself why some obscure part of his mind was asking for more than he had already.

He did not know the answer.

Yet he knew it was what he sought when he travelled the world looking, as Jason had looked, for the "Golden Fleece."

As the Duke drove away from Devonshire House, he found himself thinking of Anastasia.

He was determined that he would not see her again.

He was quite certain he would enjoy the next few days at Lynd with Lady Branston beside him.

She would prevent his thoughts from

straying to the exotic allurements that Anastasia was inviting him to sample for the second time.

"Never, never again!" he vowed.

As he spoke aloud, he was surprised at the firmness in his voice.

He went to bed, but he could not sleep.

Finally he rose at four o'clock in the morning to pull back the curtains and see the first fingers of the dawn driving away the sable of the night.

The stars were fading and there was a hazy mist along the trees in Hyde Park.

He thought how beautiful Lynd would look and had a sudden yearning for the great house and the lake in front of it.

"Why do I bother myself with the Social World when I could be riding superb horses and breathing fresh air?" he asked.

Then he thought how enjoyable it would be to be sailing in a *dhow* along an uncharted river.

Or to be travelling over the sands of the desert into what seemed to be infinity, where the sky and the sand merged as one.

As he thought of it he told himself he was being extremely ungrateful.

What more could he want than what he had already?

He pulled down the blind, closed the curtains, and went back to bed.

He forced himself to think of Lucy Branston and the promise he had seen in her blue eyes.

"She is certainly very attractive!" he murmured.

But it was still some time before he fell asleep.

The Duke set off early after breakfast to drive to Lynd, which he knew would take him two-and-a-half hours.

His Chaise, which was built for speed, was drawn by four superlative horses.

There was a smile on his lips as he picked up the reins.

Then as the groom jumped up behind, he was glad he was alone with no one to chatter to him and prevent him from concentrating on his horses.

It was a pleasure beyond words to own such superlative horseflesh.

He wondered how he had tolerated the inexpensive animals on which he had hunted when at home with his father.

He recalled the strange creatures he had ridden in different parts of the world.

Now he knew he was offered the very best livestock before anybody else, and his name was a byword at Tattersall's Sale-Rooms.

He seldom went into his Club in St. James's Street without one of his fellow-members asking if he would like to look at the horses in their stables.

If there were any he particularly fancied, they were, of course, for sale.

"I have everything!" the Duke told himself.

Amongst the pile of letters which he had opened that morning at breakfast-time there was one from his grandmother on his mother's side.

She was a very outspoken old lady who had once been a great beauty.

She expected her wishes to be granted now that she was old in the same way they had been when most men had found it impossible to refuse her anything.

She had written in her firm hand-writing:

I hear you are going to Lynd, but when you return I wish to see you. I want to talk to you about your marriage, as it is absolutely imperative that you should have a son, in fact, several, to inherit your title.

You must remember what happened to poor Desmond, who had only one child, and a sickly creature at that, who had no chance of surviving . . .

There were several other lines to the letter which the Duke did not read but impatiently put it into his pocket.

Why, he asked himself, could he not be left alone by his relatives?

He was well aware that one day, and it could be many years ahead, he might marry for the sake of begetting an heir.

But he had no intention of taking a wife who would not embellish his name and his position.

That meant suffering the utter boredom of being tied to some well-bred but empty-headed young woman.

He knew only too well he would be bored stiff within the first month of their marriage.

"I shall do what I want to do and that is to remain a bachelor!" he told himself.

He pressed his horses to move a little faster so that he could reach Lynd.

He wanted to enjoy the possession of it alone.

chapter three

Katrina looked round the Dining-Room and knew it was exactly what she had expected.

She had been entranced by Lynd from the moment they approached the drive.

Ahead she saw the great house with its wings reaching out on each side from a centre block.

On the lake in front of it moving smoothly over the silver water there were white swans.

The Duke's standard was flying on the roof against a blue sky.

The evening sun seemed to light the windows with a warm, golden welcome.

She entered the huge hall with its statues of gods and goddesses standing in alcoves.

There was a magnificent gilded staircase climbing up to a dome in the roof, and she thought that nothing could be more impressive.

Then as the Duke walked towards them in the exquisitely furnished Salon on the first floor, Katrina almost laughed.

He appeared to fit so exactly into his background.

"Welcome to Lynd," he said to Lady Branston. "I find it difficult to tell you how delighted I am to see you!"

Katrina saw the expression in her aunt's eyes and was aware that she was ecstatic at having at last, after so much preparation, reached Lynd.

She wondered if her uncle realised how much the house and its owner meant to her aunt.

Then she told herself it was just because the Duke was so important in the Social World.

There was nothing really personal about it.

Yet she could not help noticing the light in her aunt's blue eyes and the manner in which her hand lingered in the Duke's.

It flashed through her mind that if she had not known it was an impossibility, she would have thought Aunt Lucy was in love with the Duke of Lyndbrooke.

Then she told herself she was just imagining something so ridiculous.

Katrina had travelled in many parts of the world with her parents.

But she was very innocent as regards the feelings of men and women for each other, especially those in Society.

Because her father and mother were so devoted to each other and so very much in love, she had imagined that most married couples would feel the same.

She was perceptively aware from the softness of his voice and the expression in his eyes when her uncle spoke and looked at his wife that he was in love with her.

She had supposed that Aunt Lucy felt the same about him.

Then she thought this was not a moment to be critical or to examine her own thoughts.

The Duke greeted her uncle, and then her aunt said in a somewhat affected voice:

"This is Katrina, who is very, very grateful that you have been so kind as to include her in your party. She has promised me she will be no trouble, and I am sure she will find plenty to occupy her in admiring your house."

The Duke smiled as he held out his hand.

As Katrina touched him, she had a strange feeling she could not express even to herself.

It was that the Duke was somehow different from what appeared on the surface.

She then found it bewildering to be introduced to a large number of people in the room.

They were all, she realised, much older than she was, and the women were as elaborately dressed as her aunt.

They greeted Lady Branston with an insincerity which was, to Katrina, so obvious as to be insulting.

"Dearest Lucy, how *delightful* to see you, and you are looking as lovely as *ever!*"

Every word, Katrina thought, was belied by the speaker's hard and envious expression.

Then she told herself quickly that it would be a very great mistake, when she met the guests at Lynd, for her to use what her father had called her "Third Eye."

Her mother had pointed out when they were in Egypt the lump on the foreheads of the Pharaohs.

This was the secret sign of their "Third Eye."

It was their instinct and enabled them to look deep below the surface of a man or woman to find the truth.

Katrina had been intrigued by this and after that she would say to her mother:

"Using my Third Eye, I can tell you, Mama, that the man who was trying to sell you that pot this morning was a charlatan! I am quite certain it was not a treasure from a tomb, as he claimed it was, but that it was made yesterday."

Her mother would laugh and say:

"I am sure you are right, my darling, but the poor man has to earn a living somehow!"

It was her father who had encouraged her to use her Third Eye by asking her opinion of people who came to their house in Amiens.

He would then tell her whether she was right or wrong.

Sometimes she made a mistake.

But nine times out of ten she was right in what she saw, or rather what she felt, about the person in question.

It had sometimes been embarrassing.

This, Katrina thought, was one of the occasions when she should behave as a normal *débutante,* and not look into the "World behind the world."

The bedrooms into which they were shown when they went upstairs were as impressive as the rest of the house.

Her aunt, however, seemed to think it quite unnecessary that Katrina should have a bedroom next to hers.

Aunt Lucy's room was very magnificent with a huge carved and gilded four-poster bed.

It communicated with a Boudoir filled

with malmaison carnations and containing some very beautiful pictures.

Katrina's room had, to her delight, a painted ceiling like her aunt's and some Italian pictures in the same style.

The bed was draped with muslin curtains from a gold corolla suspended beneath the high ceiling.

The dressing-table, too, was draped with muslin trimmed with real lace, and the pale blue of the walls made it a very suitable room for a young girl.

Katrina wondered if she also had an adjoining Boudoir.

But she learnt when her aunt was speaking to the Housekeeper that the room next door to hers was empty.

While the rest of the guests were in another corridor.

"His Grace is on the other side of the landing," the Housekeeper volunteered.

She pointed across the balustrade which was on each side of the well which looked down into the hall.

Lady Branston must have appeared surprised, for the Housekeeper explained:

"His Grace's traditional bedroom and Sitting-Room are in the West Wing, but we were horrified to find woodworm in the panelling. While the rooms are being repaired and redecorated, His Grace has had to move out."

"What a nuisance for him!" Lady Branston said lightly.

But Katrina had the feeling she was glad he was near her.

Her trunk was half-unpacked by the time they came upstairs.

She learnt that a young maid was to look after her, supervised by an older woman who was attending to her aunt, who had brought her own lady's-maid with her.

Katrina was used to travelling with as little luggage as possible.

She longed to be able to laugh with her father and mother at the mountain of luggage which was assembled in the hall before they left London.

She was not surprised when she learnt that it was travelling in a separate carriage with her aunt's maid and her uncle's valet to take care of it.

They themselves had no encumbrances, not even the large leather box which contained her aunt's jewellery.

It was something she certainly needed, Katrina thought, when they were ready to go downstairs to dinner.

Her aunt was wearing the blue gown which the *Vendeuse* had said matched her eyes.

With it she had a set of turquoises and diamonds which might have graced a Queen.

Her tiara was certainly very striking on her golden hair.

The ear-rings were so large that they seemed almost part of the necklace which covered most of the white skin of her chest.

There was a brooch, bracelets, and a ring, all of turquoises and diamonds.

Katrina thought it would be impossible for anyone to eclipse her aunt, until she saw the other ladies and knew they were equally resplendent.

As far as she herself was concerned, she had no jewellery.

Her mother had sold the little she had when they needed more money for their travels abroad.

Also, she had always insisted on buying the best food available to keep her husband and her small daughter well.

"Compared with His Grace's other guests, I shall be very much a 'Plain Jane'!" Katrina said jokingly to the maid who was looking after her.

Then she had been ordered into her aunt's room so that she could inspect the new gown she was wearing.

"You look all right," her aunt said. "I shall be ready in five minutes, so you can wait for me in your bedroom."

As she spoke, Katrina could feel her hostility vibrating towards her.

Quickly she returned to her own room, wondering as she had wondered so often before why her aunt had such a dislike of her.

"You look lovely, Miss!" the maid had said in answer to her remark. "The flowers should be here any minute, and I often thinks they're just as good as jewels."

"Flowers," Katrina questioned.

"They're always brought round before dinner," the maid explained. "There's corsages for the ladies an' button-holes for the gentlemen."

"What a lovely idea!"

At that moment there was a knock on the door.

The maid went to open it, and, taking a tray from the footman outside, carried it to Katrina.

There were huge purple orchids, others of green and yellow, and a lot of carnations, mostly button-holes for the men.

Katrina was thinking they were all a little overpowering.

Then she saw a cluster of some very small white flowers that were quite different from the others.

The blossoms were a little larger than a daisy.

Katrina knew from her travels in the East that they were *frangipani.*

She picked them up to smell their delicious perfume, and the maid said impulsively:

"Two or three of them would look nice, Miss, on a ribbon round your neck!"

"That is just what I was thinking," Katrina agreed, "and there is some white ribbon which we can pull out of one of my petticoats."

She felt as she did so that Aunt Lucy would not approve.

But the maid fixed three tiny blooms to it and tied it around her neck.

It gave her, she thought, the finish that her white gown required.

It made her feel that her neck and naked shoulders were not unnaturally bare.

There were a number of her flowers left, and these the maid arranged at the back of her head.

It was the way the Indian women wore their flowers and which had always seemed to Katrina very graceful.

"Now you'll look prettier, Miss, than any other lady at His Grace's table!" the maid said rapturously.

"Thank you," Katrina replied, "but I doubt if anybody will notice me when their eyes are blinded by the glittering jewels and magnificent bustles of the ladies, which are like waves breaking over the rocks!"

She heard her aunt's lady's-maid knock on the door as she finished speaking.

She hurried out into the passage to find Aunt Lucy, escorted by her uncle, was already descending the stairs.

Other guests appeared to join them.

Katrina found she was right in thinking the glitter of jewels would make it impossible for anybody to look at her.

It did not worry her, it only made it easier for her to look around at everybody else, and enjoy the beauty of the Dining-Room.

The pictures, which were in gold frames, were a perfect complement to Adam's apple-green walls which were characteristic of his decoration.

The table, with its gold candelabra and gold ornaments with circles of orchids living round them, was a picture.

It would have been impossible not to admire the Duke sitting in a high-backed chair at the end of the table.

He looked, Katrina thought, as if he were "Lord of all he surveyed."

He seemed so omnipotent that she was

sure the ladies present should curtsy to him as if he were a King.

She herself had, in fact, because she thought it was correct, dropped him a small curtsy when she had been introduced.

Now she imagined how graceful they would look if all the ladies sank down in a low curtsy while the gentlemen bowed.

Then the Duke would merely incline his head and consider it beneath him to do any more than that.

She was so intent on savouring the scene that she was quite surprised when the gentleman next to her said:

"What are you thinking about so seriously? I cannot believe you are not enjoying yourself in what is undoubtedly one of the most palatial houses in England!"

"Of course I am enjoying myself!" Katrina replied. "It is exactly what I always expected a great English house would look like."

The gentleman to whom she was speaking laughed, then he said:

"You appear to be surprisingly young to be a fellow guest of what must seem to you to be a lot of old fogeys!"

Katrina's eyes twinkled.

"I cannot think the ladies, at any rate, would think that remark very complimentary!"

"No, indeed!" the gentleman confessed. "And as you have rightly rebuked me, I will do my best to polish up my compliments, starting with you. May I say you are unexpectedly lovely for anyone so young!"

"Thank you!" Katrina replied.

She was not embarrassed by the compliment.

Living in France, she was accustomed to receiving them herself.

She had also listened to her mother's beauty being lauded to the skies by almost every man who came to the house.

She remembered her mother's instructions about finding out about people and what were their interests.

She soon discovered that the man to whom she was speaking was interested in horses, as she might have expected.

He was also a collector of stamps, of which she was quite knowledgeable.

"My father collected the stamps of every country we visited," she told him.

"Then do not lose them!" the gentleman advised. "One day they will be valuable; in fact, some of them are very expensive to buy already!"

Then she had turned to the gentleman on her other side.

She had thought him reluctant to attend

to anyone but the lady next to him.

She was obviously very amusing and had made him laugh heartily ever since the meal began.

"Have you anything to say for yourself, young woman?" he enquired a little aggressively, Katrina thought.

"That depends on what subject we are discussing," she replied. "I was wondering what your interests were and thought, although I may be wrong, that you are a politician."

"That is very astute of you, if you are not cheating and somebody has already told you that I am the Secretary of State for Foreign Affairs."

He was the Earl of Kimberley, and Katrina drew in her breath.

Quickly they were talking about countries in which he was interested, many of which she had visited.

Then the lady on his other side claimed him again.

Katrina had the feeling that the Earl was quite reluctant to return back to her.

She told herself that her mother would have been pleased with her.

When the ladies left the Dining-Room, her aunt ignored her completely.

Remembering her instructions not to

thrust herself forward, Katrina was quite content to look at the pictures.

There was a variety of other treasures in the Salon where they had congregated before dinner.

There were fascinating cabinets containing collections of snuff-boxes and Dresden china for her to inspect.

She felt only a few minutes flashed by before the gentlemen joined the ladies.

While they were in the Dining-Room, card-tables had been arranged at one end of the room.

Everybody was debating whether they would play cards or talk on the comfortable sofas.

Katrina, going to one of the windows, drew back the curtain slightly.

What she saw outside made her draw in her breath.

The moon was shining in a sky glittering with stars, and the moonlight on the lake had turned it to silver.

It was so lovely that as usual she felt herself caught up in the beauty of it so that it became a part of her mind and she felt radiance in her heart.

A deep voice beside her made her start:

"I am wondering, Miss Darley, what you would like to do?"

Without even wondering who was speaking to her, Katrina replied:

"I would like to fly up into the sky towards the stars, then dive down into the depths of the silver water!"

She spoke very softly.

When the speaker did not answer, she looked around and saw it was the Duke who was standing beside her.

He was looking at her, she thought, in a very strange way.

For a moment he just looked into her eyes.

Then he said in a voice she thought had a slightly mocking note in it:

"I am glad you admire my possessions."

"The house is . . . magnificent!"

"And I hope you think it is a fitting background for its owner!"

Now Katrina knew he was definitely mocking her.

She was not to understand that it was what every woman said to him as soon as they arrived at Lynd.

He had heard it a thousand times since he had become its owner.

Then to his surprise Katrina looked again at the stars.

"I am not certain," she said as if she spoke to herself, "that it is the right background for you."

"What do you mean by that?" he enquired.

"I may be wrong, but your background should be the snow-capped Himalayas or the infinity of the desert sands under a blazing sun."

She did not herself understand why she was saying such things.

They just came into her mind and she knew she was using her "Third Eye" as she had been trying not to do.

The Duke was silent in sheer astonishment, then he said sharply:

"Who has been talking to you about me?"

"No one!" Katrina said hastily. "I am sorry if I sounded . . . rude . . . but you asked me a question . . . and I told you what was in my . . . mind."

"That is exactly what surprised me."

He was about to ask her to explain what she meant and why she had said it.

But the door of the Salon opened and the Butler, looking across the room to where he was standing, announced:

"The Earl and Countess of Calverton, Your Grace!"

For a moment the Duke felt as if he were turned to stone.

Then with an effort he walked towards Anastasia.

He realised when he reached her that she

was exceedingly alluring in a travelling-coat trimmed with sable and with feathers in her bonnet.

"My dear Duke!" she exclaimed, holding out her hand towards him. "Forgive us for being late, but it was impossible for my husband to leave London earlier."

She paused and smiled fetchingly at him.

"I told him of your kind invitation to join your party, and he is deeply grateful as he has to be at the County Show in Buckinghamshire tomorrow morning, which would have meant an exceedingly early departure from London."

The pressure of Anastasia's fingers as the Duke held them told him that she was expecting him to accept her extraordinary arrival.

He was wondering how he could protest that he had given her no invitation, when the Earl intervened:

"What my wife is trying to tell you, Lyndbrooke, is that I am going to leave her here with you and travel on to stay with Lord Buckhurst."

He paused and then continued:

"I am to be the principal judge of cattle at the County Show in his grounds, and Anastasia had said it was too far for her to journey in the middle of the night. What is more, she is not really interested in cattle, as I am sure you can guess!"

He laughed at his own joke, and then before the Duke could speak, Anastasia chimed in:

"I know I shall be safe and comfortable here with you, my dear Duke, and Lord Buckhurst's house is notoriously cold and draughty."

Again there was the firm pressure of her hand, and at last the Duke found his voice.

"I am, of course, delighted that you should be my guest."

"That is very kind of you, Lyndbrooke," the Earl said heartily. "I will be with you as soon as possible to-morrow, but I doubt if it will be before dinnertime, and now I must be on my way."

The Duke escorted him down the stairs to the front-door.

Anastasia went with them and kissed her husband an affectionate farewell.

"Enjoy yourself, my dear," she said, "and do not worry about me. If you have to stay another night to please His Lordship, I shall quite understand. Besides all his cows, he might have some decent horses!"

The Earl laughed.

"I will certainly have a look at them. Good-bye, Lyndbrooke," he said, putting out his hand. "It is very decent of you to have us."

The Earl then proceeded slowly down the steps and into the carriage that was waiting for him below.

As it drove off, the Duke turned to see Anastasia looking at him with dancing eyes.

"Am I not clever, *Mon Brave?*" she asked in French so that the servants could not understand what she was saying.

"You are outrageous, as well you know!" the Duke said. "And totally unexpected."

"You have always enjoyed the unexpected."

"My last word to you was 'No,' Anastasia."

"I heard it," she answered, "but I never, as you know, ever take 'No' for an answer!"

She laughed softly as she spoke and despite himself the Duke found that he was laughing too.

"You are atrocious," he said, "and quite incorrigible!"

"And what could be more intriguing?" she enquired.

The Duke, when he went back to the Salon, deliberately sought out Lady Branston.

As he had hoped, she showed no sign of being upset by the arrival of Anastasia.

This told him that no gossip about his relationship with the Countess many years ago had reached Mayfair.

Because he was perturbed by Anastasia thrusting herself upon him, he deliberately flirted rather more ardently with Lucy Branston then he would have done otherwise.

This was easy, because Lord Branston was at the card-tables.

They were able to walk quite naturally into the Ante-Room next door, ostensibly to look at his pictures.

"It is impossible for them to look more beautiful than you do at the moment," the Duke said, "with the turquoises matching your eyes."

"You are very kind," Lucy replied in a soft voice.

"That is what I want to be," the Duke answered.

She put her hand into his and he raised it to his lips.

As her fingers tightened on his, he knew that she was wanting him to kiss her lips.

He moved quickly to the door through which they had just come from the Salon and closed it gently.

Then he took her in his arms.

Her lips were what he had expected — eager, passionate, but at the same time controlled, as Anastasia had never been.

As the past intruded on his thoughts, the Duke kissed Lucy more demandingly.

When she responded, he went on kissing her, until she put up her hand to her hair, as if she were afraid he might ruffle it or unbalance her tiara.

"You are very, very lovely!" he said in a deep voice.

"That is what I want you to think," Lucy replied.

She drew in her breath, then she added:

"We must go back and, if it is possible, which I hope it will be, we can talk later."

The way she spoke told the Duke exactly what she meant.

Without speaking, he merely kissed her again.

He realised she was sensible in saying they could not be away for too long, and he opened the door into the Salon.

The chatter of voices greeted their ears like the twittering of an aviary full of birds.

As they walked into the room, the Duke told himself he would stand no nonsense from Anastasia.

He had told her No, and he meant No,

and she would have to accept it whether she liked it or not.

He thought Lady Branston was very tactful.

She was enthusing over the beauty of the pictures in the Ante-Room to the first people they met.

"I am exceedingly glad," she was saying, "that we have a few days in which to explore this wonderful Aladdin's cave."

"That is what I always feel when I come to Lynd," somebody replied.

Then, as the Duke moved away, Anastasia came into the Salon.

She had been amazingly quick in changing her clothes.

He remembered it was one of the more delightful things about her that she seldom kept a man waiting.

Glittering with jewels and wearing a gown that had travelled without being in any way creased, she came directly to the Duke.

"I must introduce you to my other guests," he said conventionally.

"I came to see you, and you only, Tristram!" she answered. "Your guests are a bore!"

A servant brought her a glass of champagne and she sipped it.

As she did so, she looked at him over the

rim with her seductive green eyes which he knew had a question in them.

"The answer is 'No'!"

"Could I have arranged anything better than that I should be here alone?"

"That was your arrangement — not mine!" the Duke answered.

She drank a little more champagne before she said:

"We will continue this conversation later, when your guests have retired early to bed. It is Friday night, and I am sure they are all tired."

"No, Anastasia!"

"If you do not come to me, I shall come to you! We have, *Mon Brave,* to talk about ourselves."

"There is nothing to talk about."

The Duke's eyes were hard and so was his voice, but Anastasia just smiled at him before she said:

"I will give you twenty minutes after we have all retired to bed, and if you lock your door, I shall hammer on it!"

She turned away from him with a little flounce of her bustle and a sensuous movement of her body.

It conveyed an unspoken invitation which was as dangerous as the swinging head of a Cobra.

The Duke was furious, but there was nothing he could do.

He was well aware that Anastasia would keep her threat and come to him.

Nothing could be more of a disaster than that she should hammer on his door where she could be overheard.

Too late he realised he should have told the servants when she arrived that the Earl and Countess of Calverton should be placed in a different wing from his other guests.

But he had a disturbing feeling that she would be in the empty bedroom at the top of the stairs.

It was near to the room he himself was using while the Master Suite was being re-decorated.

It was the best suite that was not already occupied, and had a dressing-room attached to it, as well as a *Boudoir.*

He was quite certain that was where Anastasia would have been installed.

"Dammit!" he exclaimed beneath his breath. "Why did I not think of it sooner."

He wondered desperately how he could convey to Lady Branston without her being suspicious that tonight she was to stay in her own room.

When the party broke up early, largely

owing to Anastasia, who announced she was tired, everybody went upstairs.

Each guest carried, as was traditional, a lighted candle that was handed to them in the hall by a footman.

The Duke was immediately aware that his supposition was correct.

Anastasia was in the "Queen Anne Room," with Lucy Branston only two doors away in the "Charles II Suite."

Nothing could have been more unfortunate, but it was too late now to do anything about it.

The Duke managed to say in quite an ordinary tone of voice to Lady Branston:

"I am sure you are tired, as indeed I am, and we will all feel better tomorrow."

But he doubted if she understood what he was trying to convey to her.

Anastasia, on the other hand, went into her room carrying her lighted candle and without speaking to him except to say goodnight.

He could see by the sparkle in her eye that she had every intention of having her own way and she had him in a trap out of which he could not escape.

He opened the door of his room to find his valet waiting for him.

He wondered if he should say he had an

urgent desire to sleep elsewhere, but knew it would cause consternation amongst the staff.

As there were so many people staying in his house, the main bedrooms in this part of the house were all occupied.

Doubtless those in the other wings or on another floor were not made up.

He knew that he could not move as easily as he might have done when he was a man of no importance.

Now a housemaid would have to be fetched to provide him with the best linen sheets.

His valet would have to move all his personal belongings, including his ivory hairbrushes, razors, shoehorn, button-hook, and comb.

His night-attire would also have to be transferred, all of which would take time and cause a great deal of comment below-stairs.

"There is nothing I can do," the Duke told himself.

He then decided he would go as quickly as possible to Anastasia's room to tell her he had no intention of staying.

He would make it even clearer than he had done the other night that, whatever they had felt for each other in the past, their intimacy was now a closed book.

It was one he had no intention of re-opening.

While he was doing that, he could only hope that Lady Branston would not come to his room as she had insinuated.

He knew old men slept very soundly, but that was not to say they went to sleep quickly.

If Lucy Branston was to leave Lord Branston, she would first have to make sure that he was in a deep sleep.

One from which it would be difficult to rouse him.

'She will not come to me, it will be too dangerous,' he thought.

At the same time, he could not be sure of anything, and it was a very unpleasant situation in which to find himself.

His valet left him and, as soon as he was alone, the Duke put on a white shirt which he took from one of the drawers.

It was not stiff like the one he had been wearing in the evening at dinner, but very much more comfortable.

With it he wore a pair of long, tight-fitting black trousers and a silk scarf which was tucked into his open-necked shirt.

He then put on a black velvet jacket frogged with braid and a pair of velvet slippers embroidered with his monogram surmounted by a coronet.

He knew it would be far wiser to talk to Anastasia fully dressed than if he was wearing night-attire.

Gently he opened the door of his room.

As he expected, there were only a few lights burning in the silver sconces.

But the great well in the hall was dark and he could only just make out the outline of the staircase.

It was impossible for a night-footman sitting in the padded chair in the hall to see what was happening on the floors above him.

Unless, of course, anyone deliberately leaned over the bannisters.

Keeping close to the wall, the Duke moved silently until he reached the door to Anastasia's bedroom.

For a moment he hesitated, thinking that he was a fool to go to her.

But it would be still more foolish to let her come to him.

In that case, however much they argued, he would not be able to escape from her.

His lips were set in a tight line as he opened the door.

As he did so, he was unaware that another door on the landing moved silently open.

chapter four

As the Duke had anticipated, Anastasia was looking very alluring.

Her dark hair falling over her shoulders, her green eyes glinting.

What amused him was that she was wearing a necklace of black pearls.

The Duke remembered that her passion for jewels made her invariably wear them even in the most intimate moments of love-making.

He was well aware that the black pearls, like her emeralds, her rubies, and many other necklaces, accentuated the whiteness of her magnolia skin.

Instead of being in bed, she was sitting on the side of it.

Her diaphanous nightgown did little to conceal the lissomness of her body.

The Duke shut the door, then, not moving towards her but standing just inside the room, he said:

"I have come to you, Anastasia, because you blackmailed me into doing so, but I have no intention of staying and, as I said before, it would be a great mistake to move the clock backwards."

Anastasia smiled.

Then she said softly:

"You are very handsome and very desirable, *Mon Cher,* and I think your position becomes you."

"You must listen to me, Anastasia," the Duke said patiently. "I appreciate that you are an extremely alluring woman, but you are now married to a very distinguished man, and you should try to behave yourself."

"I have already told you that the only person who could ever make me do that is you!" Anastasia said in a soft, seductive voice. "Do you remember, Tristram, how jealous you were and how delightfully brutal when you were incensed with me?"

The Duke moved uneasily across the room to stand with his back to the fireplace.

Although it was warm in the daytime, it was often chilly at night.

A fire had been lit, but he thought as he stood in front of it, it seemed to be giving out no heat.

"I have come to your room because you forced me to do so," he said after a moment. "Now I am going back to my own and, if you stay as my guest, I can only ask you to remember you are your husband's wife."

Anastasia threw back her head and laughed.

"Darling, how pompous you are as a Duke," she said. "I think I liked you better as a penniless young soldier."

"Whom you refused to marry!" the Duke replied sharply.

"Which was very, very stupid of me, and I realise now, bitterly, enviously, and very humbly, Tristram, what I have missed."

The Duke did not answer, and after a moment she said:

"But I am still a woman, and you are still a man, and I know if we touch each other, the fires that consumed us so ecstatically will still be burning."

"I doubt it," the Duke said dryly, "and I have no intention, Anastasia, of trying to find out!"

"But I have!" she said softly.

She rose from the bed.

As she came towards him he stood still, wondering what he should do.

He knew that if he once succumbed to Anastasia's blandishments, it would be a very great mistake both for himself and for her.

He remembered how uncontrolled, how primitive she was.

He was quite certain the Earl of Calverton would not stand any nonsense from his wife.

He would, in fact, defend his honour by every means in his power.

It flashed through the Duke's mind that the Earl would not challenge him to a duel.

That was now an out-of-date method of settling differences between a husband and a lover, although duels still occasionally took place.

But the Earl might easily divorce Anastasia, citing him as co-respondent.

It would be a scandalous long-drawn-out, and expensive case, which would have to go through Parliament.

There had been several divorces lately.

The newspapers had revelled in divulging every intimate detail of the behaviour of the guilty parties.

He could see all too clearly how they would treat him and Anastasia.

Then Anastasia reached him and held out her arms to encircle his neck.

Suddenly he knew, surprisingly, almost incredibly, that she no longer attracted him.

He could not explain it to himself, for no woman could have looked, in fact, more entrancing or seductive than Anastasia did at this moment.

Her nakedness was in no way concealed

by the transparency of her nightgown.

It revealed that she had not lost the soft curves of her up-tilted breasts, and the smallness of her waist.

She still had the slim line of her hips, which had delighted him in the past.

And yet now his body did not react in any way to her allurements.

He thought contemptuously that her effort to seduce him was of no avail.

It was finished, finished completely and absolutely.

The enthraldom in which she had held him for so long after they had parted had gone.

He had loathed and detested all women because Anastasia was in his blood and he could not rid himself of her.

He could remember the long nights when he lay tossing and turning in the heat under a *punkah* that did not work.

The heat of his own body had been agonizing because he wanted her.

She drew closer and still closer to him and the fragrance of her exotic French perfume which he remembered was in his nostrils.

Her lips were inviting his and he could feel the flames rising within her.

Yet he was as dispassionate as if he were being embraced by an icicle.

"Mon Cher, je t'adore," Anastasia was whispering the words he had heard so often and missed when she was no longer there to say them.

But his reaction now was no more than if she had asked him to pass the salt.

He raised his arm, and, taking hold of her wrists, pulled them away from his neck.

"I am sorry, Anastasia," he said quietly.

She stared at him incredulously.

"Are you telling me," she asked after a moment, "that I mean nothing to you?"

"What is past is past," the Duke said, "and it would be a mistake, a very grievous mistake for both of us, to look back."

"I do not believe you!"

She put her hands, with their long fingers which he had kissed a thousand times, against his chest.

She moved herself even closer as she said:

"Kiss me, Tristram! Kiss me and you will find you are mistaken and you want me as I want you."

The Duke took hold of her shoulders and turned her round to face the bed.

"I know you are sensible enough to realise that I mean it when I say 'No,' and I think it would be a mistake once you and your husband have left Lynd for us ever to see each other again."

Anastasia turned back, and now the expression in her eyes was very different.

"But I am not sensible! I love you, Tristram! I have always loved you! I will not let you go!"

"You may have loved me as a man," the Duke said quietly, "but you know full well it was not enough. You wanted money, Anastasia, you wanted a social position which I could not give you at the time, but which you have since attained, and now you must be content with it."

"And if I am not?" Anastasia asked. "Shall I tell you that I have never forgotten you, and I have wanted you — oh, God, how I have wanted you."

She drew in her breath before she went on:

"Now we can be together and you can love me in the same way as you loved me before."

The Duke smiled, and there was a bitter twist to his lips.

"Now you are talking like a child. Things are never exactly the same, and as far as I am concerned, they never will be."

"I will make you want me!" Anastasia answered fiercely.

She was throwing herself at him.

As he put out his hands to prevent her

doing so, someone turned the handle of the door.

It was so unexpected that both Anastasia and the Duke were still, staring at the gold handle.

By the light of the candelabrum beside the bed, they watched it twist and turn.

Then a voice which was easy to recognise said:

"It is I, Anastasia, let me in!"

The Duke looked at Anastasia and saw the expression of terror in her eyes.

If he had not been in such a difficult position, he might have laughed.

He could see how little her protestations of love meant when it came to the crunch.

"*Mon Dieu!* It is my husband!"

Her lips mouthed the words, but there was no sound.

There was a sudden loud knocking on the door as if the Earl were growing impatient.

"Let me in, Anastasia!" he called in a louder tone than he had used before.

The Duke looked round the room and saw there was a connecting door which led into a dressing-room.

He was just about to move towards it.

Then he remembered that if the Earl had returned for some unknown reason, the servants would be bringing up his luggage.

There was no escape that way without being seen.

Almost simultaneously his eyes and Anastasia's went towards the windows.

There were two in the room.

As if she begged him to do so, the Duke moved towards the one which was nearest to the wall between Anastasia's and the next bedroom.

As he did so, moving soundlessly over the thick carpet, the Earl knocked again.

Now Anastasia with what the Duke thought was a consummate piece of acting asked sleepily:

"What . . . is it? What do . . . you want?"

"It is I, Anastasia."

She gave a little cry of what sounded like delight as she exclaimed:

"Hugo!"

"Yes, Anastasia, open the door!"

She gave another cry of apparent delight as she exclaimed:

"You are . . . back."

As she spoke, the Duke went behind the curtain.

He silently pushed the square-paned Georgian window a little higher so that he could climb out onto the balcony.

In Regency times the third Duke had added wrought iron balconies to the windows at the back of the house.

Thereby not spoiling the simplicity of Adam's design of the front.

But it had made the part of the building which looked over the gardens more ornate.

The balconies were not large.

Unfortunately, as the Duke remembered as he stepped out onto the one outside Anastasia's window, it did not connect with the balcony of the room next door.

There was a gap of about three feet between them.

There was, however, nothing he could do but risk falling forty feet or more as he jumped from Anastasia's balcony on to the one next door.

He had, in fact, been a good jumper when he was at school.

But he knew with a sarcastic twist to his lips that now in the moonlight he might easily misjudge the distance.

He would then end up dead, or badly injured, on the ground below.

It was, however, a chance he had to take as he heard Anastasia open the door and exclaim in the voice of a delighted wife:

"Darling, what a lovely surprise! But what has happened?"

"I had an accident about ten miles from here," the Earl replied, "some half-witted yokel coming out of a side-turning ran into the carriage and buckled a wheel. There was nothing I could do but persuade the local Vicar to lend me his gig."

"How terrible for you!" Anastasia exclaimed. "But, *Mon Cher,* I am so grateful that you are not hurt in any way, and I was missing you, sleeping alone."

The Duke had heard enough.

He wondered how he could ever have believed in Anastasia, with her two-faced hypocrisy.

As she was talking, he had taken off his slippers.

Now, holding them in one hand, he climbed barefooted onto the iron-railing.

With his other hand against the wall of the house, he faced the adjoining balcony and supported himself.

Then, drawing in his breath, he jumped.

He landed to his satisfaction neatly in the centre of the balcony next door and put on his slippers.

He was pleased to think that the years of soft living had not impaired his athletic prowess.

He knew it would be a mistake to linger on the balcony.

By some mischance the Earl might look out of the window in his wife's bedroom.

As quietly as possible, he entered the next room.

The window was, fortunately, as wide open as it was possible for it to be.

The curtains were also pulled back and he was aware that somebody lay asleep in the bed.

As he had been trained in the Army to move silently, he thought it would be easy, with the aid of the moonlight, to cross the room.

He would reach the door without disturbing the occupant of the bed and let himself out into the passage.

He had, in fact, walked without making a sound to the centre of the room, which was quite a large one.

Suddenly the door opened and Lucy Branston entered, holding a small candelabrum in her hand in which three candles were lit.

The Duke, standing very still, stared at her as she said in a voice of shocked surprise:

"Your Grace! This is certainly a surprise! What can you be doing in here?"

As she spoke, the Duke realised for the first time that it was Lord Branston's niece who was asleep in the bed.

Her aunt's voice had awoken Katrina and she sat up.

"What is . . . happening?" she asked.

"What is it . . . Aunt Lucy?"

Her voice was very young and startled, but Lady Branston did not even turn her head.

Her eyes were on the Duke, and, seeing the fury in them, he realised quickly what had happened.

Lady Branston, if she had been to his room as he suspected she had, would have queried where he had gone.

'Women, all women,' he told himself, 'are vindictive.'

As soon as Lucy heard the Earl's arrival, she must have guessed that this room would be his only means of escape.

She was looking very alluring, and he appreciated it was for his benefit.

She wore a negligee which matched the blue of her eyes and was profusely decorated with shadow lace.

Her fair hair had been brushed until it gleamed like gold in the light from the candles.

He was aware that had he been waiting for her, as he had intended to do, he would have found her enchanting.

Now there was an anger he could only think was spiteful in her eyes.

Her lips were certainly not soft and inviting as they were when he had kissed her in the Ante-Room.

She was waiting for an answer to her question.

He said quietly with a composure he was, in fact, far from feeling:

"I am afraid I have made a mistake, for, of course, I had no idea your niece was in this room."

Then he thought he was being extremely clever as he added:

"When I heard that the Earl of Calverton had arrived back unexpectedly, I thought, rather stupidly, that this was the dressing-room he would be occupying, forgetting it was on the other side of his wife's bed-room."

"You can hardly expect me to believe that!" Lucy said acidly.

The Duke was wondering how he should reply, when behind Lady Branston appeared a bulky figure enveloped in a heavy woolen robe.

"What is going on, Lucy?" Lord Branston enquired querulously. "I was woken by what sounded like somebody knocking, and found you had left me."

For a moment there was absolute silence.

Then, before the Duke could speak, Lucy said:

"I, too, was awakened and thought the

knocking you heard, dearest, was on Katrina's door, but when I came to find out, I discovered to my utter astonishment that His Grace was here!"

"His Grace?" Lord Branston asked, coming farther into the room.

Because he had been standing behind his wife, he had been dazzled by the light of the candles she held.

He had not realised until now that the Duke was present.

"What has happened? What on earth is going on?"

He looked at the Duke as he spoke, then at Katrina.

She was sitting up in bed, her hair looking silver as it fell in soft waves over her shoulders.

Her eyes, which were always large, seemed to be even larger as she stared in astonishment at what was taking place.

"I can quite easily explain my presence," the Duke said to Lord Branston. "When I learned that the Earl had returned unexpectedly, I came to see if his luggage was being brought up to his dressing-room. I thought mistakenly it was this room instead of the room on the other side of the Countess's bedroom."

He spoke slowly and clearly, as if he were

talking to a child.

Before the Earl could speak, Lady Branston said:

"That may sound very plausible, but the fact remains that I found you in the middle of the night in the bedroom of a young and innocent girl."

As she spoke, as if she found the candelabrum was too heavy for her, she set it down on a chest-of-drawers.

"Well, of course," Lord Branston said slowly and somewhat reluctantly, "I must accept your explanation, Lyndbrooke, but I only hope nobody else knows you were here, otherwise it would be very damaging to my niece's reputation."

"I am, of course, aware of that," the Duke replied, "and I apologise very humbly to Miss Darley. I was actually half-asleep when I was informed of the Earl's arrival, and I can only think that my brain was not working as clearly as usual."

He forced a smile to his lips as he spoke and looked at Lucy Branston, hoping he had appeased her.

She was obviously, however, still very angry.

He could feel her fury and jealousy vibrating towards him across the room.

"That is all right then," Lord Branston

said. "Now let us all get back to bed and get some sleep. I admit to being extremely tired."

He turned as he spoke.

Then, as the Duke's eyes again met Lucy's, he saw a change of expression in hers which he did not understand.

It was as if she had suddenly thought of something which delighted her and had swept away her anger.

As her husband reached the door, she said in a low, soft voice:

"I think, darling, you are being rather gullible in accepting His Grace's explanation. It seems to me very strange, if he was asleep as he said he was, that he should have found time to dress himself so elegantly after being informed of the Earl's arrival."

She paused, and as he said nothing, she continued:

"That must have been only a few moments ago, because you said that the noise he was making on his wife's door woke you!"

"What are you saying? What are you talking about?" Lord Branston asked.

"You know, darling, about these things better than I do," Lady Branston said sweetly. "But do you not think the Duke should make reparation for ruining poor innocent little Katrina's reputation?"

There was a moment's stupefied silence on the part both of Lord Branston and of the Duke.

Then because the former, realising exactly what his wife was saying, said somewhat awkwardly:

"I see your point, my dear, and I am quite certain in the circumstances that Lyndbrooke will behave like a gentleman."

The Duke drew in his breath before he said:

"That is something you and I will discuss to-morrow, Branston. In the meantime, it is absolutely imperative that no one, and I repeat, *no one,* except ourselves should know what has occurred here to-night!"

He spoke with a note of authority in his voice and as he did so he looked at Lucy.

She smiled at him, but there was that same expression in her eyes that he did not understand.

Lord Branston, sounding even more embarrassed than he had been before, said:

"We will certainly talk about it in the morning, Lyndbrooke, and you are right about no gossip and nobody else knowing what has occurred."

He walked out of the room onto the landing as he spoke and, as the Duke followed him, Lucy turned back to look at Katrina, who had not said a word.

She was still sitting up in bed, bewildered by what was happening, and finding it all incomprehensible.

Lucy's eyes flickered over her, and as she saw how young she looked and how lovely, her lips tightened.

She was about to speak, but thought better of it.

Picking up the candelabrum which she had brought with her from her bedroom, she shut Katrina's door and followed her husband.

He was getting into bed.

As she put the candelabrum down on the dressing-table, she said in the soft voice she reserved for the purpose of coaxing him into doing something she wanted:

"You are quite right, Arthur, as you always are, to make the Duke realise he must make reparation to Katrina for being in her bedroom in that unfortunate manner."

Lord Branston stared across the room at his wife.

"You are surely not suggesting that he was seducing the girl?"

"Whether he was, or whether he was not," Lucy replied, "as you very well know, darling, your niece's reputation will be blackened for ever if anything becomes known of this disgraceful episode."

She paused before she went on:

"Can you imagine what would be said about any girl, however young and innocent, if it was known there had been a man in her bedroom in the middle of the night?"

"I cannot believe that Lyndbrooke, who has never seen her before this evening, had any such intention!" Lord Branston said.

"That is immaterial, darling, as I know you understand," Lucy said. "What really matters is that your poor sister's daughter will have to pay the price."

She stopped speaking to brush her hair from her forehead.

"She will be treated as a 'scarlet woman' by everybody in the Social World if it is ever whispered that the Duke was in her bedroom at one o'clock in the morning!"

Lord Branston was frowning, but he did not speak and Lucy went on:

"You are quite right, as you always are, and how I adore you for it, in saying he must behave like a gentleman. Of course he must marry her, and the sooner the better, just in case things are much worse than we think."

The shocked voice in which Lucy said the last words made it unnecessary to elaborate on what she was insinuating.

She knew from the expression on her husband's face that he understood exactly what was expected of him.

He, however, made one last stand in the Duke's defence.

"If we all keep our mouths shut — and that means you are to tell nobody, nobody, do you understand — then there is no reason why anybody should know."

Lucy laughed the silvery little laugh she had practised ever since leaving the School-Room.

"Dearest Arthur, you are so kind and always make excuses for everybody! But you must have realised, because you are so astute, that there were servants bringing the Earl's luggage upstairs."

She paused before continuing:

"They must have seen us, as I saw them as I was coming out of Katrina's bedroom. They will have thought it strange, very strange!"

Lucy made a gesture with her hand as she said:

"If one servant knows, everyone below-stairs will know by to-morrow morning, and what do you think the lady's-maids and the valets will tell their masters and mistresses?"

There was silence.

Then Lord Branston, turning heavily

onto his side, said:

"You are right, Lucy. I will speak to Lyndbrooke in the morning, but now I want to go to sleep."

He shut his eyes, but Lucy, before she blew out the candles, took a quick look at herself in the mirror.

She had been clever, far cleverer than she had ever given herself credit for.

She had contrived to get that tiresome girl off her hands.

At the same time, she had made absolutely certain that in future she would be continually welcome at Lynd.

It would not be a case, as it had been this time, of angling, intriguing, and praying for an invitation.

She knew what the Duke felt for her.

When she saw him going into Anastasia's bedroom, she had been consumed with a violent, uncontrollable jealousy, more intense than she had ever felt before.

If she could, she would have killed him for treating her in such a way.

He knew perfectly well that she was coming to his room as soon as her husband was asleep.

Now, however, there would be no need to hurry or count the hours she would be privileged to spend at Lynd.

The moment Katrina was married — and the Duke could not wriggle out of his obligation — she would make it clear to him.

He was an intelligent man, and he would realise that everything then would be far easier for them.

There would be dozens, if not hundreds, of opportunities for them to be alone together.

No one would be in the least suspicious that she was anything but a very devoted aunt to his wife.

"Nothing could be better!" Lucy told herself. "And it will certainly be the end of that over-dressed, serpent-like Countess of Calverton!"

She had sensed that Anastasia was a dangerous woman.

She had seen the way she looked at the Duke as she said good-night to him.

Lucy had nevertheless not really been afraid of her attractions until she saw the Duke going into her bedroom.

Then, if she could have murdered Anastasia, she would have done so without hesitation.

When she found the Duke in Katrina's bedroom, she was aware it was his only way of escape from the Earl.

Nevertheless, her keen eye had not

missed the neatness of his appearance.

It was not that of a man who had hurried into his clothes when the Earl had knocked unexpectedly on the door.

She had noticed that the silk scarf around his neck was unruffled.

His velvet jacket was not in any way disarranged as might have been expected.

She was, therefore, confident that Anastasia had not been successful in enticing him into her bed.

Simultaneously, Lucy had realised that her fury had suddenly melted away.

The idea which had come to her was like a light in the darkness.

Katrina was young, innocent, and, she thought, very stupid.

If she married the Duke, she herself could occupy a far more secure place in his life than she did at the moment.

As Lucy got into bed, she was aware that her husband was already asleep.

She lay in the darkness thinking rapturously of the parties she would persuade the Duke to give at Lynd.

She would undoubtedly be the most important person there.

Even if the Prince of Wales, as was likely, was included amongst the guests, she would still be supreme.

As the Duke's aunt-in-law, she would have a place in Society far loftier than what was hers at the moment.

Finally she forced herself to relax.

She must try to sleep so that she would look beautiful the next day.

As she did so she told herself that everything was perfect and the sooner the Duke and Katrina were married, the better.

It would be to everybody's advantage — especially hers.

The Duke found it impossible to sleep.

He stood at the window unaware of the beauty of the night, wondering how he could escape from the trap that had been set for him by Anastasia.

It had, however, resulted in something quite different from anything she had intended, or he had expected.

He had known from the determination in Lucy's eyes that she would put pressure on Lord Branston.

He would demand that he marry Katrina, and he could not for the moment see any possible way of escape.

He was well aware that Lucy was justified in saying that, if it was known that he or any other man had been in a young, unmarried girl's bedroom in the middle of the night, the gossips would find only one explanation for it.

It was only through marriage that the Social World would accept her.

He hoped, of course, that no one would know what had occurred.

Yet he knew of old that it was impossible to trust a woman with a secret.

Especially where it concerned himself and another woman, even in the shape of a very young girl.

"They will talk, of course they will talk!" he told himself.

He was not particularly concerned with Katrina's feelings, but rather with his own.

He had escaped marriage for so long.

This was despite pressure from his grandmother and every other relative who was old enough to tackle him on such a delicate subject.

He had no intention now, if he could help it, of marrying a girl he had seen to-night for the first time.

She was so young that they could not have any interests in common.

All this had happened because Anastasia was up to her old tricks of making him miserable.

'It would give me great pleasure,' he thought, 'to strangle her.'

He remembered the unhappiness she had caused him in the past.

Now, when his life was literally a "bed of roses," she had once again, like the wicked witch in the fairy-story, put a curse on him.

He could hardly believe it had actually happened.

"How was I ever involved with her?" he asked himself.

He knew cynically that it was a question every man asked himself at some time in his life, and he was no exception.

'I will try to get Branston to see sense,' he thought when finally he got into bed.

He knew that Lucy would be pulling in the opposite direction.

He had, therefore, little chance of behaving any other way than, as the Earl had said, "like a gentleman."

When morning came, the Duke was in a furious temper.

Those who had served with him knew he could be icily calm.

But there would be daggers in his eyes and every word he uttered would sound like the crack of a whip.

When he went downstairs to breakfast he learnt that the Earl of Calverton had left very early.

He had borrowed a carriage and horses, leaving fulsome apologies for having done so.

The Duke knew this meant that Anastasia was now alone, and he wondered how he could rid himself of her.

He left the breakfast-table before most of his male guests had appeared and was in his Study, when Lord Branston came in.

"I have to talk to you, Lyndbrooke," he announced. "Is this a convenient moment?"

"I suppose so," the Duke replied ungraciously.

He rose from the desk at which he had been reading the letters which his secretary had already opened for him.

Moving across the room, he indicated a comfortable high-backed armchair.

He seated himself in another one facing it.

He realised as he did so that Lord Branston, despite the long years he had spent at Court during his distinguished career as a Statesman, was somewhat embarrassed.

As if he felt he ought to help him, the Duke began:

"I am sorry about last night, Branston, but I think you know me well enough to be aware that I was not doing anything which could upset or injure your niece."

"Of course I take your word on that score," Lord Branston replied. "At the same time, we both know that if it ever came out that you were in her bedroom, the girl would be finished — absolutely finished as far as the Social World is concerned!"

The Duke did not speak, and Lord Branston went on:

"I was very fond of my sister. She made an unfortunate marriage to a man who was not good enough for her. But she was very happy. I have to do my best for her only child."

There was an uncomfortable pause before the Duke said:

"I presume by that you think I should marry her."

"I really see no alternative," Lord Branston replied. "As my wife pointed out, while we may keep silent about what occurred, there were servants bringing up Calverton's luggage and they will talk."

He paused a moment, then continued:

"As you and I are well aware, half the gossip that causes so much trouble one way or another comes from the Servant's Hall."

"I am afraid you are right," the Duke agreed.

There was a note of despair in his voice.

"What I am going to suggest," Lord Branston said, "and naturally it was my wife's idea, is that you and Katrina should be married as quickly as possible and go off on a honeymoon before anyone is aware that you are engaged."

The Duke stared at Lord Branston in astonishment.

"Why should she suggest that?" he asked.

Then he knew the answer even as he asked the question.

It was because Lucy, who, of course, was the brains behind all this, suspected he would try to wriggle out of it.

She was, therefore, making sure he did nothing of the sort.

"It seems to me that it is the sensible thing to do," Lord Branston said as if he were working it out for himself.

He was, in fact, remembering what his wife had said.

"Katrina has just been bereft of her father and mother," he went on, "so it would not be surprising that you do not want a big wedding."

He stopped talking a moment, then continued:

"Secondly, if, as we must anticipate, people learn what has occurred, they must wonder whether or not she is having a child. You could prevent this happening by being married immediately."

Lord Branston paused, then he said in a genial tone:

"I am thinking of you, Lyndbrooke, as well as of my niece."

"Thank you," the Duke said cynically, knowing his sarcasm would be lost on the Earl.

"You have a Chapel here, and I suppose a Chaplain," Lord Branston continued. "You should, therefore, be able to organise everything so that there is as little talk about it as possible. Once the marriage is a *fait accompli*, what can people do about it?"

"What indeed?"

The Duke was consumed with a fury that made him speechless.

Keeping himself under a super-human control, he walked to the window to stare out at the sunshine on the lake.

He told himself he had had five years of happiness at Lynd.

Now, when he least expected it, it was to be snatched from him.

He would have to share everything with a tiresome, ignorant girl.

She would doubtless think of nothing but the fact that she was a Duchess and could deck herself out in the family jewels.

He wondered if he should go off on his own and travel as he had done in the past to strange places.

Perhaps while he was away everything

would blow over and be forgotten.

As he thought of it, he could recall last night seeing Lucy's expression suddenly change.

From one of vindictive fury and jealousy it became something different.

Because he was extremely astute, he knew the answer.

He would not only be marrying Lord Branston's boring niece.

He would also be marrying Lucy, and to Lucy her ambitions were of paramount importance.

Instead of the green lawns sloping down to the lake, the yellow irises surrounding it, the water shimmering in the sunshine, all he could see were three women menacing him.

They were, he told himself, ruining his life.

Anastasia, with her green eyes glinting with a fiery desire.

Lucy, the conventional beauty, seducing him with a secret smile.

Beside them the faceless, unimportant girl who would be his wife.

He saw them holding him prisoner, fettering him with the chains of matrimony.

He longed for the power to fly away from them on a magic carpet.

It would carry him to the other end of the

world, where they would never find him.

Instead, because he was a Duke, because he dare not, when it came down to "brass tacks," offend or insult Lord Branston, he would have to do exactly what was required of him.

He turned from the window.

In a quiet, conversational tone which was admirably controlled he said:

"I will, of course, do as you suggest, and when my other guests have left on Monday, I will arrange for my marriage to take place immediately."

chapter five

When her uncle and aunt and the Duke had left the room, Katrina tried to understand what had happened.

She could hardly believe that the Duke had entered her room through the window.

Nor could she understand why he should have done so.

It seemed to her completely incomprehensible.

It was even more astonishing that her Aunt Lucy was so angry about it.

She had said such strange things which had made the Duke furious.

Because Katrina was so perceptive, she had felt his fury coming from him in waves.

She was also aware that her aunt was being spiteful and bitter in a way she did not understand.

She had listened to the conversation among the three of them, which seemed, incredibly, to concern herself.

She still could not work out what was happening until she realised that her aunt thought it extremely reprehensible of the Duke to be in her room in the middle of the night.

Katrina knew this was true.

But she was aware that he had not been in the least concerned with her.

He was, when her aunt entered, walking so quietly towards the door that he had not awakened her.

Why? she asked. Why should he have come into her room through the window?

Because she was so puzzled, she got out of bed and drew the curtain back even farther.

She then looked out of the open window at the stars and the moonlight.

For a moment their beauty made her almost forget everything else.

Then she was aware that there was a light coming from the window next to hers, and she could hear voices.

At first she thought it strange that anyone should be speaking. The Countess of Calverton had gone into the next room alone.

Now she could hear a deep voice.

She remembered that the Duke had spoken of the Earl having returned unexpectedly.

Like a jigsaw puzzle falling into place, Katrina knew the only way the Duke could have come into her room.

It was possible if he had jumped from the Countess's balcony onto hers.

It was then that she recalled the Countess Anastasia arriving unexpectedly after dinner.

She had come downstairs surprisingly quickly in an evening-gown, bejewelled and looking like somebody out of a story-book.

Katrina had found it difficult not to stare at the Russian because she was so unusual.

Then the Countess had slipped her arm through the Duke's and turned her strangely beautiful face up to his.

As she did so, Katrina had thought that, like her aunt, here was another woman who was in love with him.

Yet she was puzzled that he should have gone into the Countess's bedroom.

Then he had left it by jumping from her balcony onto the one next door, which was hers.

What was he doing?

What was he saying to her that he could not have said downstairs?

Then the answer came to her.

Not only was the Countess in love with the Duke but he also was in love with her.

Suddenly she pulled the curtains to shut out the beauty of the stars and the moonlight on the garden.

She knew as she got back into bed that she was shocked, very shocked.

How could anyone so magnificent and important as the Duke be in love with another man's wife.

"It is wrong," she told herself, "very wrong, and Mama would tell me not to think about it."

However, try as she would, it was impossible not to see the Duke's handsome face.

He was more good-looking than she had ever imagined a man could be.

The Countess's green eyes had been looking at him in a way which at the time Katrina had thought was embarrassing.

Now she knew it was wicked.

Then she was back to the question which had puzzled her from the start, as to how she personally was involved in this drama.

The Duke had explained that he had come to her room by mistake.

If it was true that he was merely seeing to the Earl's luggage, why should there be any secrecy about it?

And why was Aunt Lucy making such a fuss because inadvertently he had entered her bedroom?

Then Katrina could hear her aunt saying:

"Do you not think the Duke should make

reparation for the way he has besmirched poor innocent little Katrina's reputation?"

There had been a moment's silence, Katrina recalled.

Then her uncle, in what she thought was a somewhat embarrassed manner, had said:

"I am quite certain in the circumstances that Lyndbrooke will behave like a gentleman."

What did that mean?

What would "behaving like a gentleman" entail?

It all seemed to repeat itself over and over again in a twisted fashion in Katrina's brain.

She was still puzzled when she fell asleep.

Katrina awoke early.

Although she wanted to get up and go out, she thought perhaps it was something she should not do without her aunt's permission.

She had learnt from the maid who looked after her that while the gentlemen breakfasted downstairs, the ladies had their breakfast in their bedrooms.

"I expected, Miss," the maid said, whose name was Emily, "you'd be up a bit earlier if you're goin' to watch th' Point-to-Point."

"Point-to-Point?" Katrina asked in surprise.

She had heard about Steeple-Chases and Point-to-Points from her father, but had not expected to see one at Lynd.

" 'Is Grace allows it on 'is own race-course, Miss, an' it's ever so excitin' for them as lives 'round here."

She saw Katrina was interested and went on:

"It's not the same as the Steeple-Chases 'Is Grace gives later in the year, an' which 'e take part in 'imself, as do 'is friends. But the Point-to-Point is for everyone who's got a 'orse. Th' farmers challenge each other and the crowds cheer their favourite, an' it's fun — it really is!"

"I do hope I can watch it!" Katrina exclaimed.

"I'm sure you'll be able to, Miss. 'Is Grace is th' judge and gives away th' prizes 'imself, or gets one of th' ladies in his house-party to do it."

Katrina was sure it was something she would enjoy.

She only wished her father could be with her to explain it all, as she knew he would have done.

When she had finished her breakfast, she dressed quickly.

She put on what she thought would be a suitable gown, and the plainest bonnet she possessed, before going downstairs.

She had learnt from Emily before doing so that her aunt had not yet been called.

She therefore hoped she had a chance somehow to get to the Point-to-Point before prevented from doing so.

Katrina reached the hall.

She saw there was a brake outside into which a number of gentlemen were climbing.

There were also half-a-dozen horses being held by grooms obviously waiting for their riders.

Lord Kimberley, whom she had sat next to at dinner the previous night, saw her first and exclaimed:

"Are you coming with us, Miss Darley? I expect it will be a long time before we are joined by the other ladies in the party."

Katrina smiled at him.

She remembered how much she had enjoyed their conversation at dinner.

"I should love to come, if you think it will be all right," she replied.

"It is always right to do what you want to do," the Earl answered, "and ask permission afterwards."

There was laughter at this, and one gentleman said:

"It is all very well for you to talk like that,

Kimberley, but there would be the very devil to pay if it happened in your Ministry!"

"There certainly would!" the Earl agreed. "However, I think it is a good idea that Miss Darley should join us, and we can all take the blame if she gets into trouble for doing so!"

There was more laughter.

Katrina, making up her mind, climbed into the brake and sat down beside the Earl.

"I hope you slept well," he remarked as the brake started off.

"Yes . . . thank you," Katrina replied.

She felt a little shiver go through her just in case the Earl or anyone else had any idea what had happened last night.

They reached the Duke's private racecourse which was not far from the house.

She saw a large number of horses and riders gathered there and a lot of spectators.

There were children getting in the way of the riders.

There were dogs, some obstreperous, some walking sedately beside men who Katrina guessed were shepherds.

There were also a large number of men wearing what she supposed was the Duke's livery, who were probably game-keepers.

It was particularly fascinating because it was exactly what her father and mother had told her took place in the English countryside.

Especially on estates that were owned by rich landlords.

She walked beside Lord Kimberley as he went up to the riders who were taking part in the Point-to-Point.

He inspected their horses and talked to the owners.

He was pleasant as Katrina remembered her father had been to the labourers in the village in which they had lived.

Then suddenly all heads turned in one direction.

She saw the Duke come riding towards the Starting-Point on a black stallion.

He was accompanied by six of his guests also on horseback.

He was, however, so magnificent that Katrina knew it would be difficult to look at anybody else.

There were murmurs of: "Mornin' Your Grace!" and "Nice to see Your Grace!" from men in the crowd as well as those on horseback, who doffed their hats to him.

The Duke acknowledged their salutes.

Then he rode in front of the riders, turning his horse so that he could address them.

In clear authoritative tones he told them

the rules of the race.

He reminded them that on their return they had to circle the race-course before passing the Winning-Post at the end of it.

Katrina watched the horses moving to the starting points and wished she could take part in the race herself.

But there were no lady-riders.

The wives and sweethearts of the young farmers and other men taking part were there just to cheer them on.

The Duke then moved to one side as the riders formed themselves with some difficulty into a line.

After the most refractory horse had been brought under control, the Duke fired a starting-pistol into the air.

They were off.

They rode away into the countryside, and the Duke and other gentlemen on horseback followed them to see that they kept to the course.

As they moved off, Katrina found it difficult to watch anybody but the Duke.

Then she was aware that two open carriages had arrived.

One of them contained her aunt and several other ladies.

In the second the Countess of Calverton had one of the ladies and two other gentlemen with her.

The Earl and the gentlemen got out and walked to join the Earl of Kimberley, who was inspecting a jump on the race-course.

Katrina was wondering whether or not she should go to her aunt's carriage, when she saw the Countess beckon to her.

For a moment she thought she was mistaken.

Then she realised it was an imperious gesture she could not ignore and hurried to the carriage.

When she reached it, the Countess said sharply:

"Get in! I wish to speak to you!"

It was impossible for Katrina to refuse.

A footman opened the door for her and she stepped into the carriage and sat on the back seat beside the Countess.

Anastasia was looking even more fantastic, she thought, than she had the day before.

She was dressed entirely in emerald green, with a silk gown trimmed with lace and velvet ribbons.

Her small bonnet sported quills of the same colour, and she would have been outstanding in Rotten Row.

Besides being flamboyant, she was also extremely beautiful.

Katrina felt she could understand why the Duke was so attracted to her.

Anastasia, on the other hand, thought that Katrina was too insignificant to be of any interest.

Yet she badly wanted to find out what had occurred the previous night.

She had been aware that there were voices coming from the room next door.

It had gone on long enough for the Earl to change from his travelling-clothes into his night-attire and return to her before they ceased.

She therefore said quite pleasantly to Katrina:

"Do tell me what was happening in your bedroom last night. I could hear quite loud voices and they prevented me from going to sleep."

Katrina drew in her breath.

She remembered how the Duke had said that no one was to speak of what had occurred, and she wondered wildly what she should reply.

Then because she was quick-witted she said:

"I think when your husband knocked on your door he awoke Aunt Lucy and Uncle Arthur."

"If that is what happened, it must have

been very tiresome for them," Anastasia remarked, "but I cannot understand why they should have gone into your room."

"I think Aunt Lucy thought I might be frightened and Uncle Arthur followed her."

There was silence, and as Katrina looked away at the crowd moving about on the race-course, Anastasia said:

"Was anybody else with you?"

This Katrina knew only too well was a dangerous question.

She avoided answering it by pointing to where at the side of the race-course there was a gaily-coloured caravan.

"Oh, do look!" she exclaimed. "There are gypsies and I have always hoped to see them when I was in England! I wonder if there is anyone who would take me to speak to them?"

She did not wait for the Countess to reply, but opened the door of the carriage herself before the footman could do so.

She jumped down onto the ground.

Not daring to look back at the Countess, she hurried to where she could see Lord Kimberley.

When she reached him, she found him deeply engrossed in talking about horses.

She listened but did not interrupt by speaking of the gypsies.

She felt, however, that she had dealt quite competently with what had been a dangerous moment.

She had no wish to disobey the Duke.

There was, however, no chance of speaking intimately with anyone.

The Point-to-Point took up much of the morning.

When the race had been won, the prizes were presented not by Lucy or Anastasia, but by the elderly wife of the Lord Lieutenant.

She had arrived just as the leading rider was taking the last fence in style.

After that there was a large luncheon-party in the house.

They were late sitting down and did not leave the Dining-Room until it was nearly four o'clock.

The ladies went upstairs to change their gowns for tea. Lucy followed Katrina into her bedroom and shut the door behind her.

Katrina looked at her aunt questioningly as she said:

"I saw the Countess of Calverton speaking to you at the Point-to-Point. What was she saying?"

"She asked who was talking here in my bedroom last night," Katrina answered.

"And what did you tell her?"

"I said that you and Uncle Arthur had

been woken up by hearing somebody knocking on a door, and thought I might be frightened."

"That was intelligent of you," Lucy said. "You did not mention that the Duke was also there?"

"No . . . of course . . . not!"

Lucy thought for a moment, then she said:

"Keep away from that woman, she is dangerous, very dangerous, although, of course, she has done you a good turn."

Katrina looked puzzled.

"What do you mean by that?"

"You cannot be so half-witted," Lucy said scathingly, "as not to realise that if it had not been for the Countess, you would not now be marrying the Duke!"

Katrina stared at her aunt as if she could not believe what she had heard.

Then she asked in a voice that did not sound like her own:

"D-did you say . . . m-marry the D-duke?"

"Of course you are going to marry him! Do you not understand that as your uncle and I found him in your bedroom, there is nothing he can do to save your reputation except make you his wife!"

"It . . . it cannot . . . be true!" Katrina faltered.

"Oh, for Heaven's sake!" Lucy said irritably. "Do I really have to explain to you in words of one syllable that if anyone — anyone at all — had the slightest idea that the Duke had been in your bedroom at one o'clock in the morning, you would be ostracised by every decent woman in the Social World?"

She paused to give an affected little laugh as she added:

" 'It is an ill wind that blows nobody any good,' but as far as you are concerned, it has blown you a coronet with strawberry leaves!"

"B-but the . . . Duke did not . . . realise this was . . . my r-room!" Katrina stammered.

"That has nothing to do with it," Lucy replied. "I found him here, and he will marry you! And if you ask me, you are a very lucky young woman!"

"I will not . . . marry him!" Katrina said quickly. "He is . . . in love with . . . somebody else and I could not . . . possibly marry . . . any man who did not . . . love me!"

Lucy looked at her with such an expression of contempt that instinctively Katrina took a step backwards.

"Then all I can say is that you are even more of a fool than I thought you were! Good heavens, Katrina, this is the luckiest thing that could possibly happen to you!"

Her voice rose as she went on:

"You will be the Duchess of Lyndbrooke, and although I had intended to find you a husband as quickly as possible and get you off my hands, I never aspired as high as a Duke!"

"B-but . . . Aunt Lucy . . . you must listen to me . . . " Katrina began.

"I am not going to waste my time," Lucy interrupted.

"Your uncle is arranging everything, and as he is your Guardian, you know that by law you have to obey him. You will marry the Duke, no matter what he wants or you want, and the sooner the better!"

Then as if she had nothing more to say Lucy opened the door and stalked out of the room.

She left Katrina staring after her as if she had been turned to stone.

It was something she had never expected in her wildest moments.

She thought the Duke was the most magnificent and impressive man she had ever seen in her whole life.

But she knew that no marriage could be based on any foundation except love.

If he was in love with the Countess of Calverton, then he would have no wish to become involved with her.

He would hate the idea of having a wife whom he did not love.

She could remember the anger vibrating from him last night.

If that was what he felt, it would be unthinkable for her to live with him.

"I must . . . speak to him! I must . . . tell him it is . . . impossible!" she told herself.

She wondered if he would understand.

The ladies all came down to tea rather late, wearing lovely and very elegant gowns.

The gentlemen, too, had changed out of their riding-clothes, and tea was served in the Orangery.

This had been added to the house only fifty years ago.

From it had come the beautiful orchids which Katrina had admired last night.

She could, however, think of nothing but the Duke and how she could tell him what she felt.

But he never looked in her direction and was always deep in conversation with someone else.

At dinner she found herself seated at the far end of the table.

There were so many extra guests that there was no chance of speaking to him.

She was, however, aware when the ladies left the Dining-Room that her Aunt Lucy and the Countess were being offensive to each other.

They spoke in soft, sweet voices which belied the enmity in their eyes.

Katrina guessed that they hated each other and knew perceptively that it had something to do with the Duke.

That was something she did not wish to express in words, even to herself.

There were card-tables ready, as there had been the night before.

There was also music from a String Orchestra playing in another Reception Room beyond the Salon, where they could dance if they wished.

Katrina danced with two or three gentlemen in the party, then with several younger men who had come to dinner.

When the Duke had made no effort to come near her or speak to her, she finally slipped away.

She went to bed before Lucy made any move to do so.

As she lay in the darkness she could only pray to her father and mother, begging them to tell her what she must do.

"How can I marry anyone . . . Mama, who does not love . . . me as Papa loved you?"

she asked. "And because he has been . . . forced into marrying me, the Duke will . . . hate me. How could I live in this house, knowing he has . . . no wish for . . . me to be here and wanting . . . somebody very . . . different in . . . my place?"

It was, of course, impossible for the Duke to marry the Countess.

At the same time, Katrina thought that even though it was wrong, it would be very wonderful to be loved by him.

She told herself it was all a hopeless mess.

She felt frightened and with no idea what she could do about it, she found the tears running down her cheeks.

As she tried to wipe them away, she heard Aunt Lucy's bedroom door shut.

A little later there were sounds on the other side of her room.

This told Katrina that the Countess of Calverton had also retired to bed.

When she thought how beautiful she was, and how alluring with her green eyes and white skin, Katrina felt her tears become a tempest.

She wept until she was exhausted.

The Duke went to his Study after deliberately having had breakfast early so as not to encounter any of his house-party.

He had already been out riding, finding it impossible to sleep.

He knew that only by taking strenuous exercise could he relieve his depression and his anger.

He was still furious.

Not only with Anastasia who, he told himself bitterly, might be expected to mess up his life for the second time, but also with Lucy.

Without her interference, he knew he could have persuaded Arthur Branston, who was a kindly man at heart, to forget what had been an extremely unfortunate incident.

He knew that Lucy's jealousy had made her intent on trapping him from the moment she realised he was with Anastasia.

That she had been successful made her, he thought, beneath contempt.

He could only hope that once he was married to her niece, he would never have to see her again.

He knew exactly what she expected after the marriage had taken place.

He told himself that on that score, if on nothing else, she would be disappointed.

He was still hoping that a miracle would save him.

Although what it could be he had not the slightest idea.

To-morrow when his other guests would have departed he would have to contact his private Chaplain and arrange his wedding.

He wondered what would happen if he said point-blank that he utterly refused to marry Katrina.

If he told Branston, who expected him to "behave like a gentleman," to go to hell?

Had he been only Tristram Brooke, he knew it was something he could have done.

But Lord Branston, with his position at Court, could make things very unpleasant for him as the Duke of Lyndbrooke.

In fact, he could create a scandal which would affect the whole family.

Only yesterday the Lord Lieutenant's wife had told him after she had presented the prizes that her husband intended to resign at the end of the summer.

"He thinks, my dear Duke," she had said, "that you will perform the duties, for which he is now too old, to the benefit of everybody in the County."

"You are very kind," the Duke murmured.

"I am speaking the truth," the Lord Lieutenant's wife had assured him, "and you know that my husband, if he is well enough, will help you in any way he can."

That was just one of the things Lord

Branston could prevent happening.

There were many other ways the Duke knew in which he could make life for himself and his family extremely uncomfortable.

"I shall have to go through with it," he told himself despairingly.

At that moment the Study door opened.

He looked up impatiently because he did not wish to be disturbed, and saw Katrina standing there.

Surprised, he rose to his feet.

She walked up to the desk at which he had been sitting and dropped him a little curtsy.

Then she said in a small, rather frightened voice:

"C-could I . . . talk to . . . Your Grace?"

"But of course!" the Duke replied.

She sat down on the hard chair in which he usually interviewed his Manager or a servant.

He did not suggest that they move to anything more comfortable, but seated himself opposite her.

There was silence, as if she sought for words.

Because he realised that she was frightened, he said:

"Perhaps I should apologise to you for what happened the night before last."

"N-no . . . please . . ." Katrina said quickly.

"There is no . . . need to do that. I . . . I understand what . . . happened and it was very . . . brave of you to jump from one . . . balcony to the other. You might have . . . fallen."

"I was rather pleased to find that I could do it safely."

Again there was a pause, and Katrina said:

"Aunt . . . Lucy has . . . told me that I . . . have to . . . m-marry you . . . but I have . . . another idea . . . if you will . . . listen to it."

"Of course I will listen," the Duke answered, "but I think there is no alternative except to do what your uncle and aunt wish."

He could not help his voice sounding sarcastic.

As he saw Katrina's eyes flicker, he thought perhaps he had been cruel to the child.

"What I was . . . going to suggest," Katrina said, the words coming a little jerkily from between her lips, "is that if you will . . . give me a little money . . . just a little, I . . . could go abroad and . . . disappear."

The Duke stared at her as if he could hardly believe what he had heard.

"I presume you have somebody in mind to accompany you?"

"Nobody," Katrina said, "but . . . I will go away . . . if I can afford to . . . do so."

"And where would you go?"

"I expect if I . . . returned to France where I lived with Papa and Mama . . . before they died . . . Uncle Arthur would . . . follow me . . . but I was thinking of . . . other places where he would . . . never find me."

"Such as?" the Duke enquired curiously.

Katrina hesitated, then she said:

"When we were in . . . India there were some Nuns working in Calcutta . . . amongst the poor. I could help them . . . with the . . . children."

The Duke stared at her, thinking that he could not have heard her right.

She went on, almost as if she were speaking to herself:

"In Cairo, Mama and I visited an . . . Orphanage which was desperately short of . . . women to help them and . . . I could perhaps look after the . . . smaller children there."

"Are you saying that you have been in India and Egypt?" the Duke asked in surprise.

"I have . . . been to many countries with . . . Papa and Mama . . . and it was very exciting."

She paused a moment as if remembering the past:

"We were very poor so did not travel comfortably . . . but we got to know many . . . strange and different people . . . and I know that I should feel far more 'at home' among . . . them than I do with . . . Aunt Lucy's friends."

She had been about to say "your friends," but thought it might seem rude and therefore changed it.

But her hesitation was not lost on the Duke.

"You have certainly surprised me!" he said. "I had no idea you had lived anything but a somewhat restricted sort of life because your father and mother were not rich."

"You might have thought it restricting, seeing how much you own," Katrina replied, "but in France we knew all sorts of different people who came to see Papa because he was an artist and who admired Mama because she was so beautiful."

She paused and then continued:

"Our house seemed always to be filled with people who had all sorts of exciting and different interests and love."

She said the last word almost beneath her breath.

The Duke knew without her telling him that she was afraid of the future.

A future in which there was no love such as she had known with her father and mother.

"I suppose you know that I have been to India?" he said after a moment.

"I thought you might have gone there with the Regiment in which you . . . served," Katrina replied.

"I also went back again after I had left the Regiment," the Duke said.

Katrina gave a little sigh.

"I have never known anybody who has been to India who did not long to return, and that is why I would be quite happy there . . . if you could possibly give me the fare . . . to . . . Calcutta . . . and I am quite . . . prepared to go . . . steerage."

"Alone?"

The word seemed to echo round the walls and Katrina said:

"I should be . . . all right."

"How could you possibly be sure of that, looking as you do?"

She did not understand for a moment, then she said:

"You mean . . . there might be . . . men who would make . . . things . . . difficult for me?"

"I think that is putting it mildly, especially the way you are suggesting you should travel."

Katrina made a little gesture with her hand.

"If you . . . want me to . . . disappear . . . it does not matter how I do so."

"I did not say I wished you to disappear," the Duke reminded her, "it was your idea."

"It is what I must do . . . rather than make you . . . miserable and . . . unhappy."

"You do not think that being a Duchess would compensate for being married to me?"

She looked away from him.

He realised there was something different about her profile than he had noticed in any other woman.

It struck him that her straight little nose was classical.

In her very young, childlike face it made her beauty different in a way he could not explain.

He bent forward and leaned his arms on the desk so that he could clasp his hands together as he said:

"Does the idea of being my wife really disgust you so much?"

"No . . . no! It is not . . . that!" Katrina said quickly. "I think you are . . . magnificent and . . . different from any man I have ever seen . . . but I know you are in love with . . . somebody else and . . . I could not . . . bear that you should hate me and wish every day you were not married to . . . me."

The Duke was astonished.

"Who said I was in love with anybody?" he enquired aggressively.

He saw Katrina's eyes flicker.

He knew without asking any further questions what she was thinking.

He realised it was inevitable that was what she would think and wondered why he had not considered it before.

After a short pause he said:

"I think, Katrina, if you and I are to be married, it would be a mistake for there to be any secrets between us. We should make a pact, here and now, that we will always tell each other the truth."

Katrina drew in her breath.

"I would never . . . lie to . . . you," she said in a low voice.

"I promise you the same," the Duke replied, "and therefore, so that there need be no more misunderstandings between us, I want you to know that when I came to your room from the Countess's, I had not, as you may be thinking, been making love to her."

He saw the colour slowly diffuse Katrina's cheeks and thought it made her look very beautiful.

"It was . . . wrong of me to . . . think such a thing," she said humbly.

"No, it is what anybody would have

thought under the circumstances. The truth is that the Countess is an old friend whom I knew many years ago. We were very close to each other then; in fact, I asked her to marry me, but she refused."

"She . . . refused?" Katrina exclaimed.

"I was an impoverished Subaltern, with no prospects of becoming a Duke, who could hardly afford to keep myself, let alone a wife."

He paused before continuing:

"While the Countess, as you can imagine, wanted all the comforts that a rich man could give her, and a position her beauty deserved in the Social World."

The Duke spoke sarcastically, and Katrina listened intently.

"I had not seen her again until we met in Devonshire House the night before I came down to Lynd for this house-party. She then arrived here uninvited, believing we could pick up the threads of our old intimacy!"

Katrina's large eyes were on the Duke's face as he went on:

"Because it was impossible to speak to the Countess downstairs, as there were so many people to overhear, I went to her room to tell her that as far as I was concerned, she no longer had any place in my life."

As the Duke spoke, he was thinking of

that strange moment when he realised Anastasia no longer had the power to captivate him.

He had been free — free of the ghosts and memories that had haunted him.

As he finished speaking, he looked at Katrina and realised there was a different expression now in her eyes.

He could only describe it by saying there seemed to be a light behind them.

Without moving, without saying anything, she seemed suddenly to have come alive.

She glowed, there was no other word for it.

She had a radiance that made him feel she was not human, but part of a dream.

Then as their eyes met and they looked at each other, Katrina had the strange feeling that they met across eternity.

Unexpectedly the door suddenly opened and the Earl of Calverton came into the room.

"So here you are, Lyndbrooke," he exclaimed. "The servants told me you were in your Study."

The Duke turned slowly, almost reluctantly, to face the Earl.

Katrina felt as if she had suddenly come back to earth with a bump.

The Earl walked across the room.

"I hope I am not interrupting anything," he said. "If I am *de trop,* you must tell me so."

Katrina got to her feet.

"I am sure . . . Aunt Lucy will be . . . awake and wanting me," she said a little incoherently.

Then she slipped from the room without looking back at the Duke.

He had the strange feeling that the sunshine had gone with her.

chapter six

The Duke arrived at the Church with Lord Kimberley.

He was not really surprised to find that the only other member of the house-party present was Katrina.

He saw her looking very young and fresh in the huge carved family pew.

As he did so, he realised it had been a long time since any of his fashionable guests had appeared at Church on a Sunday.

It was traditional for the Duke to read the lessons when he was in residence.

He had done what was expected of him, although he often thought it was a bore when he might be riding.

Today, however, the Secretary of State for Foreign Affairs had sent a message to say that if he was going to Church, he would like to accompany him.

The two men had driven in an open carriage to the Church which lay in a corner of the Park.

As they drove along under the shade of

the great shady oaks, Lord Kimberley had said:

"A very amusing party, Lyndbrooke! I have enjoyed myself immensely!"

"I am delighted," the Duke replied.

"Incidentally, that niece of Branston's is the most charming and intelligent young girl I have ever met."

The Duke looked surprised.

The Earl was well-known as being extremely fastidious.

He was also so dedicated to his work that there had never been a breath of scandal or gossip about him.

He had never been connected with any of the beautiful women who had made it quite clear that they admired him.

"It is a pity Branston never had a son," Lord Kimberley went on, obviously following his own thoughts, "and I doubt if he will have his niece to compensate for long. She will undoubtedly be married very quickly, but she has the brains of a man."

The Duke did not reply because at that moment they arrived at the Church.

The Vicar, who was also his private Chaplain, was waiting in his surplice to lead him up the aisle.

The family pew, finely carved, was in the Chancel.

After what Lord Kimberley had been saying about her, it somehow seemed to the Duke right and fitting that Katrina should be there.

At the same time, he wondered why, as she was so beautiful, it should be necessary, if the Earl was to be believed, for her also to be clever.

The Service was soon over; the Duke had made it quite clear from the start that it should not last over an hour.

The carriage was waiting to drive them back to the house, and Katrina went with them.

She would not look directly at the Duke, which was unlike her.

It made him aware that she was thinking of the conversation they had had earlier in the day which had been interrupted.

This had made her shy.

He thought it was attractive and something he had not encountered for a long time in any woman.

Because she was sitting next to him on the back seat of the carriage, he found himself very conscious of her closeness.

He guessed that she also was aware of him.

It was not anything she said or did, and she certainly did not fawn upon him as

Anastasia would have done.

But, just as Katrina had been aware of his vibrations, he was aware of hers.

He knew they were different from anything he had felt with other women.

Katrina talked in a natural manner to the Earl, and they immediately began a discussion on the various religions she had encountered on her travels.

Listening, the Duke thought it was the sort of conversation he himself would have expected to have with the Earl.

Or any other man who was knowledgeable about the East.

What Katrina had to say surprised him, especially when she said:

"I always think, as Papa did, that the Christians make far too much fuss about death. After all, Christ made it quite clear that He came to show the world there was resurrection."

She paused a moment before she went on:

"Yet we mourn excessively, especially the Queen, who has never discarded the black crêpe she put on when the Prince Consort died."

Lord Kimberley laughed.

"That is *lèse-majesté*, but I agree with you, my dear, and a year of mourning is far too long."

"Especially," Katrina said quietly, "when we know that the person we are mourning is alive and probably laughing at us."

"Do you really believe," the Duke interposed, "that your father and mother are alive at this moment?"

"Of course they are!" Katrina said positively. "I felt them near me just now when I was in Church, and I am quite certain they will help me about any . . . problem and . . . tell me what to . . . do about it."

The way she spoke told the Duke that the "problem" she was thinking of concerned himself.

He thought that later in the day they must continue their talk.

He must make it very clear there was no question of her going abroad or trying to hide.

There were guests for luncheon, and afterwards the house-party wished to go driving.

There were several "Beauty Spots" on the estate which the guests were always taken to see on Sundays if the weather was fine.

There was a pool in the woods which was reputed to have magical powers of curing rheumatism.

There was a "Folly" from which there was a view over the whole countryside.

Also what the male members of the party especially enjoyed were the paddocks.

There the mares with their newly-born foals could be seen and appraised.

When they returned to the house it was time for tea.

The Duke thought with satisfaction that he had managed to evade both Anastasia and Lucy by sending them in different vehicles from the one he drove himself.

Anastasia was the last to arrive back.

He was just wondering where she and the two young men with her were, when he saw the carriage coming up the drive.

He quickly disappeared into his private Sitting-Room.

He had not joined the party for tea.

When Katrina went upstairs to dress for dinner, she knew she had missed him.

"I must talk to him before to-morrow," she said. "There must be some way he can avoid having to marry me . . . unless possibly he . . . wishes to do . . . so."

She thought it was exceedingly unlikely that he would wish anything of the sort.

Yet she knew deep in her heart there was the hope that if the marriage was unavoidable, perhaps one day he would love her a little.

"Just a little, Mama," she said to her

mother, "because I know that unless he hates me . . . it would be very . . . exciting to be . . . with him."

She knew that when he was in the room she was acutely conscious of him.

When they were driving back from the Church, she had been acutely conscious of him beside her in the carriage.

She had in consequence found it hard to concentrate on what the Earl of Kimberley was saying.

Or though he was not aware of it, to answer him intelligently.

"The Duke is so magnificent," she said to her mother. "How could he possibly be . . . interested in me? Yet it would be very . . . wonderful to be with him and to . . . listen to him."

She put on the prettiest gown she possessed, which, being white, was correct for a *débutante.*

It was decorated with tiny bunches of forget-me-nots.

There was a blue sash around her small waist which joined with her bustle, and she might have stepped out of a picture.

"You look lovely, you do really, Miss!" Emily exclaimed as she finished dressing her, "an' I thinks if we add some Indian flowers we have over from last night, you could wear 'em with a bow of blue ribbon and it'd look ever so nice."

The *frangipanis* not only looked pretty, but their sweet fragrance made Katrina feel very romantic.

She went downstairs to dinner hoping the Duke would admire her.

When she entered the Drawing-Room she found she was early and there were only a few people there.

Her eyes met the Duke's, and for a moment neither of them could move.

Katrina felt her heart beating frantically in a strange manner she did not understand.

Then while she was still looking at the Duke, her eyes very wide and shining, he thought, like the stars in the sky, several members of the house-party on the other side of the room laughed.

It broke the spell.

Katrina turned away, but she found it impossible to speak.

Only by looking blindly at a picture on the wall could she manage to be so self-effacing that no one noticed her.

During dinner she was conscious only of the Duke at the head of the table.

Afterwards, when the ladies left the room, she went to one of the windows at the far end of the Salon.

Slipping behind the curtains, she stood looking out into the night.

She felt the moon and stars were telling her something, but she was not certain what it was.

Then once again she was vividly conscious, as she had been in the Church, that her father and mother were near her.

She felt happy and not so afraid as she had been the previous day.

"To-morrow everybody will be leaving," she told herself, "then I can talk to him."

Because it was Sunday there was no dancing.

Nearly everybody settled down at the card-tables.

Katrina thought it would be easy for her to slip away unnoticed and go to bed.

She went from the room and walked up the stairs without taking one of the candles that were waiting on a table in the hall.

She had arranged with Emily that she would ring when she came up to bed so her bedroom, when she entered it, was empty.

There were two candles burning on the dressing-table.

She pulled back the curtains to look out at the stars and, as she did so, to her surprise the Countess of Calverton came into the room.

"I see you are going to bed early," she said, "which is what I also intend to do. But I wonder if you would do something for me first?"

"Yes, of course," Katrina answered.

She was surprised at the pleasant manner in which the Countess was speaking.

She had ignored her both yesterday and today.

"I have done something very silly," the Countess was saying. "I feel embarrassed to ask one of the servants, but I was looking out of my window at the stars, as you were, when I dropped my bracelet."

She gave a little laugh as she went on:

"My husband will be furious with me for being so careless, but I know it has fallen down just below the window, and if it is in a flower-bed, I hope it will not be broken."

"So you want me to fetch it for you?" Katrina asked.

"Would you be so kind?" Anastasia answered. "But do not go through the front hall, otherwise the servants may be curious and have something to say about a rich woman throwing her jewels about!"

She laughed again and Katrina said:

"I will go down the side-staircase and out through the garden-door. I know where it is."

"You are kind," Anastasia said, "and I feel ashamed at being so foolish."

Katrina ran along the passage and down the side-staircase.

She had discovered it when she had come down early to talk to the Duke in his Study.

She had noticed then there was a door which opened onto the Rose Garden at the back of the house.

She thought that when she had time, she would like to explore the garden and, if possible, alone without a lot of people chattering.

'Everything about Lynd is so beautiful!' she thought. 'And people talking and laughing only spoil the atmosphere.'

She found the garden-door and it was easy to unlock it, and to pull back the bolt.

It was not dark outside because the light from so many windows cast a golden glow on the ground.

But when she reached the part of the building where her bedroom and the Countess's were, she found it was dark.

There were impenetrable shadows which made her feel it might be difficult for her to find the bracelet.

She walked on until she was directly beneath the Countess's window.

Then she stood still and looked up to see

exactly where the bracelet might have fallen.

As she did so, something heavy and dark was thrown over her head.

Before she could scream or struggle, she was lifted off her feet by a man who, holding her tightly in his aims, carried her swiftly away.

It was so unexpected and a terrifying shock.

The rug, or whatever it was that covered her, was so thick, that for a moment Katrina found it hard to breathe.

Then the man carrying her started to run, jogging her up and down, so that it was impossible for her to make a sound.

'What can be happening? Who is doing this to me?' Katrina wondered frantically.

Unexpectedly the man stopped.

There was a murmur of voices although she could not hear what they said.

Then she was thrown roughly down on what she thought was a floor before wheels started to move beneath her.

She knew then that she was in a vehicle of some sort, drawn by a horse.

Bewildered, and at the same time desperately frightened, Katrina lay still.

She could feel the wheels revolving beneath her and she knew that the horse drawing the carriage in which she lay was moving quickly.

She sat up and attempted to remove the rug from her head.

As soon as she felt it with her hands she realised it was a horse-blanket.

It was why it had been so effective in silencing her and also why it had felt so heavy.

She pulled it and found that she was in darkness except for a flicker of a light.

This came from high up on what seemed to be a wall beside her.

Then she suddenly knew, even though it was too dark to see anything clearly, that she was in a gypsy caravan.

"But . . . why?" she murmured.

Were these the gypsies she had seen on the racecourse? If so, why had they wanted to kidnap her?

It was so incomprehensible that for a long time she sat where she was, trying to collect her thoughts.

She was stunned by what had occurred and she was feeling very frightened.

Then, as she reached out her hands, she found what she supposed was a bed on one side of her.

Groping round, she thought there was another on the other side and she was lying between the two on the bare wooden floor.

But why? For what purpose had she been carried away?

It was something she could not understand.

Because she was frightened it was hard to breathe, let alone think.

She pulled herself up from the floor and sat down on one of the beds.

The mattress was hard, but there was a blanket on it and a pillow on which the occupant could lay his head.

Tentatively she moved forward to feel with her hands that the front of the caravan had been firmly shut.

She thought it was bolted from the other side, where she supposed the person who was driving the horse would be sitting.

She suspected there was no other exit.

There were windows high up on each side of the walls, and when she stood up she could look out.

She could see that they were moving through a wood amongst the trees, and she could glimpse the stars.

She wondered if it would be any use hammering on the door and screaming for help.

Then she told herself sensibly that if she did that, they would either pay no attention to her or else silence her.

She therefore moved back to the bed

and sat down on it.

There was nothing she could do except pray and hope that her prayers would be answered.

After a while, because it was more comfortable, she lay down.

She knew from conversations she had had with gypsies in the past that their caravans were clean and sacred and would be burned when they died.

She laid her head down on the lumpy pillow and was aware that it smelled of sweet herbs.

She thought afterwards there must have been something soporific about the pillow.

Amazingly, after she had lain still for a little while, she fell asleep.

Katrina awoke to find daylight coming through the windows of the caravan, and it had come to a halt.

She was wondering what she should do when the door at the front opened after she had heard the bolt being drawn back.

Then there was first a young girl with dark hair and dark eyes peeping in at her.

A moment later she could see an older man who was quite obviously a Romany with his black hair falling on either side of his high cheek-bones.

They stared at Katrina, who knew she must look very odd in her evening-gown decorated with forget-me-nots.

"You hungry?" the girl asked.

"Yes, I am," Katrina replied, "but can you tell me why I am here?"

The girl looked at the man behind her and he said in a deep, rather rough voice:

"We told take you to London."

"To London?" Katrina repeated in surprise. "Why should you want to take me to London?"

He gave her a look with his dark eyes which she did not understand and said:

"Ask no questions! Best you not know! Get food."

He shut the door of the caravan as he spoke and Katrina heard the bolt go back into place.

There was nothing she could do about it.

Then as she thought about what he had said, she was so frightened that she felt her teeth begin to chatter.

Her whole body trembled with a fear which she did not understand.

When Katrina had gone down to find the bracelet, Anastasia shut her bedroom door and rejoined the party in the Salon.

Nobody appeared to have noticed her

absence because she had not joined any of the card-tables.

She had, in fact, been in another part of the Salon when she saw Katrina leave.

Now she moved slowly and with her usual grace towards the fire-place.

Then, aware that the Duke was talking to one of the young men with whom she had been driving in the afternoon, she went to the card-tables.

The Earl had just won a hand at Bridge, and was extremely pleased with himself.

The young man to whom the Duke was speaking said:

"I am surprised, Your Grace, that you are so generous as to allow gypsies on your estate! My father has forbidden them so much as to set foot on ours, and in consequence we very seldom have any game-birds poached or find that our chickens are missing."

"Perhaps you have been unlucky with your gypsies," the Duke replied. "On this estate we have always offered the Romanys hospitality, and I have never had any really serious complaints from my keepers, or, for that matter, from the farmers."

He paused and then continued:

"Also we find them extremely useful during the harvest, when usually we are short-handed."

"Then you are lucky," the man to whom he was speaking replied, "but we live near the New Forest and sometimes there is trouble with fights between rival gangs."

The Duke knew there had been no trouble at Lynd.

He rather liked the picturesque appearance of the gypsies and thought their caravans added charm to the English countryside.

He had seen gypsies in India who were metal smiths living in black tents.

Their women wore more jewellery on their arms and ankles than any other Indian women.

He decided it was a subject he would discuss with Katrina sometime.

When he thought of her, he looked round the Salon and realised she must have gone to bed.

It was after one o'clock in the morning before those playing cards had lost or won enough and were ready to retire.

One or two of the older couples had left early.

There was still, however, quite a procession of guests going up the grand staircase carrying their lighted candles.

"Good-night, Countess," Lucy said when they reached Anastasia's bedroom.

"Good-night, Lady Branston," Anastasia replied.

There was no doubt that while her voice was polite, her eyes were hard.

She realised how beautiful Lucy looked with the candlelight glinting on her golden hair.

Lucy went into her own room and her lady's-maid, who was waiting up for her, rose to her feet, stifling a yawn as she did so.

"You're very late, M'Lady," she said reproachingly.

She lifted the sapphire and diamond tiara from her mistress's hair.

"That is true," Lucy replied, "and I am tired, Agnes, so I will sleep late to-morrow."

"Very good, M'Lady."

She undid the necklace also of sapphires and diamonds and put it away in its case before she said:

"Did Miss Katrina come upstairs with you, M'Lady? Her maid who's been looking after her was surprised that she was so late considering she's gone to bed early every other evening."

"Miss Katrina went to bed hours ago!" Lucy replied. "I saw her slip away and thought she was being sensible."

"Well, if she wasn't in the Salon, M'Lady, she's not come upstairs. I goes into her bedroom just now because the maid were worried about her."

"I cannot understand it!" Lucy said.

It flashed through her mind that Katrina might be with the Duke.

But he had been playing cards at the next table and she had tried, without avail, to attract his attention.

She was almost certain that everyone else in the party had come up to bed at the same time as she had.

The Salon had been empty when she left it.

"You must be mistaken!" she said aloud.

Taking off her bracelets, she rose, and putting them into Agnes's hands, she crossed the room and opened the door.

She went into Katrina's bedroom.

She found the young maid who looked after her standing at the window.

"Miss Katrina's not come upstairs, M'Lady! I were waiting for her to ring and, when she didn't, I comes to see if she's gone to bed without my help. But, as Your Ladyship can see, it's not been touched!"

"I do not understand it!" Lucy exclaimed. "If she has gone into the garden, she will find it very chilly at this time of the night."

Then she told herself it was Katrina being tiresome as usual.

Heaven knew, the girl had been a headache ever since she had come to England.

At the same time, she had an uncomfortable feeling that Katrina might have run away.

She had been so positive that she would not marry anyone unless she loved him.

Her upbringing abroad, Lucy thought, had given her foolish ideas about marriage that no sensible English girl would have.

"Well, wherever she is, she will come upstairs sooner or later!" she said to Emily.

"You had better go to bed and leave her to look after herself. She is used to it!"

"I don't like to do that, M'Lady!"

Lucy shrugged her shoulder.

"That is up to you," she said. "Personally, I am going to bed."

She went out of the room and saw the Duke coming up the stairs.

She knew he must have gone down again probably to fetch a book, as he was carrying one under his arm.

Because she was so pleased to see him, she waited until he reached the top of the stairs.

She was thinking, as she had so often thought before, that he was the most attractive man in the whole of Society.

Once he was married to that stupid niece of her husband's, it would be very exciting to be alone with him when she stayed at Lynd.

She had already decided which bedroom she would make particularly her own.

More important than anything else was to keep the Duke as interested in her as he was the night they had first arrived.

It was impossible not to think of his kisses without feeling a little thrill run through her.

As he reached the top of the stairs, she said in a soft voice which she knew all men found attractive:

"We have had a delightful evening, and I hope you won at cards."

The Duke smiled.

"I am glad you enjoyed yourself."

"I think Lynd is the most beautiful house I have ever seen in my life," Lucy murmured, "and exactly the right background for its owner!"

There was a flirtatious expression in her blue eyes, but the Duke would have passed on to his own room.

Just at that moment, however, Lord Branston's valet came out of the dressing-room.

Through the open door Arthur Branston saw his wife standing with the Duke on the landing.

Wearing his thick dressing-gown, he came towards them, saying as he did so:

"What has happened? Is anything wrong?"

Lucy gave a little laugh.

"No, of course not, dearest, I was just saying good-night to our kind host."

Then, realising her husband would think it rather strange that she should be out of her bedroom, she explained:

"Katrina seems to have disappeared, and her maid is worried about her, but I expect she is in the garden, staring at the moon!"

"Your niece is not in bed?" the Duke queried. "But I saw her leave the Salon a long time ago!"

"So did I," Lucy replied, "and I was sure she was tired."

"It seems very strange that she is not here," the Duke said, "and if she is outside and the doors have been locked, she might not be able to get back into the house."

"I am sure we need not worry about her," Lucy said lightly.

"I can hardly imagine she is outside," the Earl interposed. "It is a quarter-to-two in the morning! It will be cold, and what on earth could she be doing all that time?"

It suddenly struck the Duke, remembering the conversation he had had with Katrina, that she might have run away.

But if she had done so, how would she manage without money?

From the way she had spoken this morning, he was sure that she did not possess any.

Without making any explanations, he went to Katrina's room and said to Emily, who curtsied when she saw him:

"Will you look and see if any of Miss Darley's clothes are missing?"

Emily looked surprised, but she opened the wardrobe door.

After a quick glance inside where Katrina's evening-gowns had been hung on one side of it and her day-clothes on the other, she said:

"No, Your Grace, there's nothing missing as far as I can tell, except for the gown Miss Katrina was wearing when she went down to dinner!"

"What about a cape or a coat?" the Duke persisted.

"No, Your Grace, everything she brought with her is here."

The Duke went out of the room and onto the landing, where Lucy and Lord Branston were waiting, without speaking.

"She must be in the garden!" Lucy said.

"Really, I have never heard of anything so tiresome! If nothing else, she will catch a cold, and that is something I have no wish to have at the moment!"

The Duke was not listening.

He went down the stairs, and when he reached the hall, he told the night-footman to open the front door.

Because everyone in the house-party had been seen to go upstairs, it had already been locked and bolted.

Now, as he obeyed the Duke's instructions, he remarked:

"I'm sure there's nobody out there, Your Grace."

"You did not see Miss Darley go into the garden?"

"No, Your Grace. She went upstairs hours ago and the Russian lady went with her."

The Duke frowned before he asked:

"You are quite certain?"

"Quite certain, Your Grace! The Russian lady followed Miss Darley up the stairs an' I hears t'em talkin'."

"Thank you, James," the Duke said. "You can lock the door again."

He went back upstairs.

Without making any explanations to Lucy or to Lord Branston, who were still on the landing, he went to the door of Anastasia's room and knocked.

After a few minutes the door was opened by her lady's-maid, who was French.

She curtsied when she saw the Duke, and he said:

"I wish to speak to your mistress!"

The maid went back into the room.

Anastasia, wearing a very provocative *négligée,* was sitting in front of her mirror with her dark hair flowing over her shoulders.

She had heard what had been said and, getting up, walked towards the Duke.

She deliberately let her *négligée,* which was worn over a transparent nightgown, fall open as she did so.

"You want me?" she enquired as she reached the door.

There was an obvious innuendo behind the words which he did not miss.

"I understand you came upstairs with Katrina," he said sharply. "You were talking to her and I want to know what you said."

There was just a little hesitation before Anastasia replied, and the Duke waited, his eyes on her face.

"I cannot remember exactly what it was," she told him. "We laughed and talked about the party, I think."

She paused and then continued:

"Then I came downstairs because the child said she was going to bed."

It sounded very plausible, but the Duke knew she was lying.

"You are quite certain she said she was going to bed?" he persisted.

"That is what she told me," Anastasia replied, "and why should I question it?"

"No, of course not," the Duke agreed. "But strangely enough she has not gone to bed, and she is not in her room!"

"How extraordinary!" Anastasia exclaimed. "That must be very worrying for her aunt!"

She moved past the Duke as she spoke, deliberately touching him with her body as she did so.

Then, walking up to Lucy, she said:

"I am so sorry for you, dear Lady Branston! It must be very worrying to have to chaperon such a beautiful young girl and keep her from getting into trouble."

"I do not imagine my niece is in any trouble whatsoever!" Lucy answered sharply. "But she is not in her bedroom and apparently, from what I have just overheard, you were the last person to see her."

"I certainly saw her," Anastasia agreed,

"but she told me she was going to bed, and I returned to the Salon."

"It certainly seems very extraordinary!" Lord Branston said heavily.

"Perhaps you are all 'making a mountain out of a mole-hill,' " Anastasia suggested, giving him a fascinating smile.

"Girls will be girls, and perhaps sometimes they are naughty! You will find she has come back safe and sound by the morning — at least one can only hope so!"

Anastasia was putting on an act, the Duke knew.

At the same time, she was being as offensive as she dared to Lucy.

As if to annoy her even more, she put her hand on Lord Branston's arm as she said:

"I think it very sweet and touching of you, My Lord, to worry about your niece, and, of course, if she is lost, we will have to search for her."

She spoke with so much feeling in her voice that Lord Branston said:

"That is very kind of you, very, but we must not keep you up now."

"No, of course not," Lucy said sharply. "We must all go to bed, and I shall certainly scold Katrina in the morning for giving us all such a fright!"

The Duke, without saying anything,

walked down the stairs again.

This time, when he told the servant to open the front doors again, he went outside.

It was not as cold as everybody had anticipated, but the night seemed dark despite the stars.

He walked along the front of the house knowing that if there was anybody down by the river, it would be difficult to see them.

Then moving round to the west wing, he went into the Rose Garden which Katrina's window overlooked.

Again it was difficult to see very much.

He walked across the grass nearer to the house, then stood looking up at the two lighted windows side by side.

Looking at Katrina's balcony and window, he saw that just as on the night he had entered her bedroom the curtains were drawn back.

"What can have happened to her?" he wondered. "Where can she be?"

He had the feeling that while she was still perturbed by the idea of their being married, the fear and horror of it which had been there at first had gone.

He remembered what he had felt as they had driven back together from Church.

He, too, was perceptive and aware of

people's feelings and what they were thinking.

He was convinced that what she felt for him had changed.

In fact, although they had said nothing, there was something between them.

It was very different from anything he had known before.

"Nothing can have happened to make her run away," he told himself, "and how could she leave anyway, without any money and wearing only an evening-dress?"

It was then he saw something on the ground and automatically bent to pick it up.

As he did so, he was conscious of a sweet scent he recognised.

Then he knew that what he held in his hand were the *frangipani* flowers that Katrina had worn at the back of her head.

He had thought that they became her far more than any jewels could have done.

It was difficult to see in the half-darkness.

Yet he was almost certain that what he held in his hands were not all the blossoms she had worn at dinner.

He remembered they were attached to the silver of her hair by a blue ribbon.

What he held between his fingers had been broken off from the main stem and, he thought, roughly.

He was quite certain now that when he took the flowers into the light, he would see they were bruised.

He knew then, as if somebody were telling him so, that something violent had happened to Katrina.

Something which he knew was wrong, and yet there was nothing to substantiate it.

He looked down on the ground.

It was too dark to see if there were footsteps or an indication that somebody had been with her.

As he walked slowly back to the house, he was puzzled and at the same time very worried.

Then as he passed the garden-door on his left, he saw that it was open.

He thought this was either an incredible oversight on the part of his staff, or else it had been opened by Katrina herself.

That would explain why the footman had not seen her leave the house.

He pushed the door farther open, as if it would tell him what had occurred.

Then with a strange feeling he did not understand, he wondered if Katrina had arranged to meet somebody, of course a man, in the garden.

In order to do so she had pretended to go to bed.

If a man had held her in his arms, he could quite easily have dislodged the flowers in her hair.

Or perhaps she had struggled against him and they had fallen to the ground.

The Duke walked into the house, leaving the door unlocked and unbolted in case Katrina wanted to come in later.

He knew as he did so that he had no wish to lose her.

In fact, whatever the explanation of her disappearance, he would find her.

He would bring her back to Lynd — and to him!

chapter seven

The Duke, finding himself unable to sleep, rose early.

Without ringing for his valet he dressed himself in his riding-clothes and walked downstairs.

The servants, who were just coming on duty, looked at him in surprise.

The maids in their mob-caps bobbed a curtsy while the footmen bowed.

The Duke, deep in his thoughts, walked past them through the front-door and round to the stables.

There he found the stable-lads cleaning out the stalls.

He said more on impulse than because he had been thinking about it:

"Which of you was with the Countess of Calverton yesterday afternoon?"

There was a short pause before one of the older lads who was called Ramon replied:

"Oi was, Yer Grace."

The Duke looked at him and remembered hearing that his father was a gypsy who had got one of the village girls "into trouble."

The illegitimate boy had been brought up by his grandparents.

Only because they had been employed at Lynd for so many years was Ramon, when he grew older, finally taken on in the stables.

It soon became apparent that he was extremely efficient with horses.

The Head Groom had once said to the Duke:

" 'E's got a touch o' gypsy magic about 'im where four-legged creatures be concerned!"

Looking at Ramon now, the Duke remembered that Anastasia had arrived back later than anybody else.

As the thought flashed through his mind, he said:

"Did Her Ladyship stop anywhere on the way back from the Folly?"

"Aye, Yer Grace, we stopped by th' gypsies."

"For what reason?"

The question was sharp, but Ramon replied:

"Oi thinks 'Er Ladyship wanted t'ave 'er fortune told."

"So she spoke to one of the gypsies alone?"

"Aye, Yer Grace."

The Duke was just about to speak again, when he saw a horse being brought from one of the stables.

"Who is that for?" he enquired.

The groom who was leading the horse answered:

"The Earl o' Calverton, Yer Grace. 'Is Lordship said as 'e wanted to ride early 'cause 'e'll be leavin' fer London 'bout noon."

The Duke made up his mind with the quickness that had made him a very successful soldier.

"Have Conqueror at the front door within half-an-hour," he said to Ramon, "and choose another horse for yourself which can keep up with him."

Ramon looked surprised.

But he merely touched his forelock and the Duke walked back to the house.

He went to his Study and sat there thinking with an expression on his face that was frightening.

He did not move until he knew that breakfast would be ready in the Breakfast-Room.

Because some of his guests were early risers like himself, breakfast was a meal which began at seven o'clock.

It continued until quite late in the morning.

When the Duke walked into the Breakfast-Room, which was just receiving the first rays of the morning sun, he found it empty.

Five minutes later the Earl of Calverton came hurrying into the room.

"Good-morning, Lyndbrooke!" he said. "I rather expected I would find you the only person down."

"You are early, Calverton!" the Duke remarked.

"I wished to ride one of your excellent horses before we returned to London. I hope you do not mind?"

"I am delighted you appreciate them," the Duke replied.

The Earl helped himself from one of the heated silver dishes on a side-table before he said:

"It has been an extremely enjoyable party, and I hope I can return your hospitality in the near future."

The Duke did not reply, and the Earl, seating himself comfortably next to him at the long table, said:

"I am afraid I rather interrupted your *tête-à-tête* with that charming niece of Branston's."

The Duke was silent, and the Earl went on:

"As I said to Anastasia, I would not be

surprised, seeing how attractive the girl is, if our most elusive Duke loses his freedom!"

He laughed at his own joke and the Duke, pushing back his chair, said abruptly:

"Enjoy your ride, Calverton. Your horse is waiting for you outside, and he is rather frisky."

"That is what I like!" the Earl said with satisfaction.

The Duke left the Breakfast-Room and walked quickly but with dignity up the main staircase.

When he reached the landing where his own room and Anastasia's were situated, he glanced around.

Because it was so early it was very quiet, and he was certain none of the ladies had yet been called.

He opened the door of Anastasia's bedroom and found, as he expected, that the room was in darkness.

He turned the key in the door behind him and walked across the room.

He pulled back the curtains of the window from which he had escaped to the balcony of Katrina's room on Friday night.

The sunshine poured in, and, as it did so, Anastasia awoke.

She would have turned petulantly away

from the light if she had not seen the Duke there.

For a moment she stared at him incredulously before she exclaimed:

"Tristram! What are you doing here?"

The Duke walked to the bed, and as Anastasia raised herself against the pillows, he sat down beside her.

There was a question in her eyes as he did so.

"I want you to tell me," the Duke said slowly, "what you have paid the gypsies to kidnap Katrina and where they have taken her."

The question was so unexpected that Anastasia could only stare at him.

Then her eye-lashes flickered.

He thought there was a touch of colour on the magnolia skin of her cheeks as she said:

"I do not know what you are talking about."

"I give you exactly one minute to answer my question," the Duke threatened. "Otherwise I intend, Anastasia, and I am not joking, to throttle the information out of you!"

Anastasia gave a little shriek of horror.

"You are mad! You have no right to speak to me like this! Go away!"

The Duke put up his hands.

Before she could prevent him, he put

them one on each side of her long neck.

As he did so he said quietly:

"You told me you liked me when I was brutal. Well, now I intend to be very brutal."

She looked at him in horror as he continued:

"I shall not only hurt you, Anastasia, but if you drive me too far, I shall merely strangle you."

His voice deepened.

"I shall not kill you, but as you may know, if your eyes go blank, it means you will have suffered brain damage from which you will never recover!"

Anastasia made a sound that was almost a shriek before she said:

"How can you say such things? How can you of all people be so cruel to me?"

"It is you who are being cruel," the Duke replied. "Where is she?"

He tightened his fingers on her throat as he spoke.

Although she tried to tear them away, she began to splutter and choke.

"Where is she?" the Duke repeated, loosening his hold a little so that she could speak.

"I — I do not — know."

The words came jerkily from between her lips.

Once again the Duke's hands were like a clamp, and he saw the terror in her eyes.

"Tell me!" he demanded.

He loosened his hold again, but now she could only gasp for breath against her pillow.

The Duke ran down the stairs and was still running as he went down the steps outside.

Ramon was waiting, holding Conqueror.

He was the magnificent black stallion the Duke had ridden for over a year, and beside him was Juno, a chestnut which was almost as speedy.

The Duke leapt into the saddle, and, as Ramon mounted Juno he said:

"Our journey is a matter of the utmost urgency, and you must show me the secret route the gypsies take to London."

For a moment Ramon looked astonished.

Then as the Duke surged ahead, going towards the race-track, which he guessed was where the gypsies had started from, Ramon followed him.

He was thinking as he did so that he had never seen his master looking so grim or indeed so angry.

Katrina was very frightened.

The gypsy girl whose name, she knew, was Lilyi, because she had heard the man calling to her, had brought her some food.

When she had also asked for some water to wash in she had returned with a bowl.

She set it down on the floor and put a clean towel on one of the beds.

After she had washed her hands and face, Katrina looked with dismay at the creases in her expensive white gown.

She found at the same time that the *frangipani* flowers in her hair were crushed and bruised because she had lain on them.

She thought, too, that there were rather fewer of them.

There had been quite a lot when Emily had arranged them in her hair last night before dinner.

She picked the petals up and put them in a corner of the caravan.

Her hair was hanging loose over her shoulders. She tidied it as best she could without a brush or a comb.

When Lilyi came back, she thought from the sounds outside that the gypsies were preparing to move on.

"Please . . . speak to me," she pleaded. "I am very frightened . . . at being here . . . without knowing where I am going . . . or why you have . . . taken me away."

She spoke in her soft musical voice.

It was the way she would have spoken to a child or anyone she was trying to coax into being friendly.

Lilyi was pretty, with large dark eyes and black hair.

She looked at her apprehensively, then said:

"I told not speak you."

"That is rather unkind," Katrina said. "We are two girls together, and why should we not talk to each other?"

Lilyi was looking at Katrina's gown, and she said:

"Very pretty! You very pretty!"

"And so are you!" Katrina said warmly.

She sat down on one of the beds and said in a low voice that could not be heard outside:

"Tell me where you are taking me?"

Lilyi looked frightened.

"It wrong!" she said. "Very wrong, but lady give fifty pounds take you 'way."

"Fifty pounds?" Katrina repeated wonderingly.

She was thinking Anastasia must hate her very much to spend such a large sum of money in getting rid of her.

"And where are we going?" she asked after a moment.

Lilyi put up her hands as if protectively.

"I not tell, it wrong, very wrong! But want new caravan an' new horse, an' fifty pound pay everythin'!"

"If you take me back," Katrina suggested quietly, "I know my uncle would give you a hundred pounds."

Lilyi's eyes widened. Then she said:

"No — no! If go back, my father taken by Police. When we sell you we get ten pound — perhaps fifteen."

As if she were afraid she had said too much, she went out of the caravan, closing the door behind her.

A few minutes later Katrina heard the horse being put back in the shafts.

Once again they were moving slowly but relentlessly towards an unknown future.

She sensed rather than understood it was something terrifying.

Looking through the small windows in the caravan, she was aware that most of the time they were proceeding through woods.

Sometimes on cart-tracks in barren, isolated land, where there was no sign of any human habitation.

She had often heard of the secret routes by which the gypsies travelled.

How they could move about the

countryside without anyone knowing they were there.

Now she thought despairingly that even if the Duke came in search of her, which she doubted, he would be unable to find her.

She knew it was the Duke she wanted.

Only the Duke would be clever enough to prevent her from being sold, whatever that might mean.

Vaguely at the back of her mind, although she found it hard to remember, she thought she could recall something her father had said.

It was when they were in Algiers.

He had been angry because English girls were shipped abroad and taken to slave-markets, where the Arabs bid for them.

She had supposed that they wanted them as servants.

It seemed strange that they should require English girls when there always seemed to be hundreds of Arab boys begging for work.

There were, too, many women in their enveloping garments who would do any menial task that was required of them.

So why should they want her?

It was a question she kept asking herself.

At the same time, she was afraid of the answer, or even guessing what it might be.

Why should anyone want to pay for her services?

Because there was nothing else to do, she lay down on the bed to pray.

She tried to feel that her father and mother were near her and begged them to help the Duke to find her.

While her uncle might be upset at her disappearance and would undoubtedly make a fuss about it, Aunt Lucy would be relieved.

She would not stir a finger to bring her back.

That left only the Duke.

As she thought of him, so strong, so athletic, so commanding, she prayed that he would be interested enough in her to try to find her.

It was a challenge which he might find irresistible.

"Send him . . . Papa! Please . . . send him!" she prayed. "I love him and even if he does not . . . marry me and he finds some way to . . . avoid having to . . . make me his . . . wife . . . I shall still . . . love him, now and for the . . . rest of my . . . life!"

She was sure she was like her mother, who had loved one man and one man only in her life.

"After having once seen your father," she had said to Katrina, "how could I ever find another man attractive? Even if every Adonis in the world knelt at my feet, I would be unable to notice them!"

Her mother had spoken with a rapt expression on her face.

It had made her look even more beautiful than ever.

Katrina had answered with a little smile:

"That is how Papa feels about you."

"Oh, darling, we are so lucky," her mother had said, "and that is the love which I pray you will find one day when you are older, which is the only true happiness in the whole world."

"That is . . . how I love . . . the Duke, Mama," Katrina said now, "but . . . as he does not love me . . . our marriage will never be the . . . same as yours and . . . Papa's."

Then she gave a little cry of terror which was like that of an animal being tortured.

She knew there would be no marriage to the Duke.

She would be sold for some unknown reason to some anonymous person, and the Duke would be free.

Free as he wanted to be, with no tiresome wife forced upon him.

Katrina covered her face with her hands.

As the tears seeped through them, she knew that all this had happened because the

Countess loved the Duke.

Even if he were no longer interested in her, there would be dozens of other beautiful alluring women to take her place.

The horses plodded on.

Once again the caravans came to a standstill and Katrina heard the horses being taken from between the shafts.

They were set free to find food for themselves.

Then she smelt smoke and knew that the gypsies had lighted a fire to cook their midday meal.

She seemed to remember hearing that gypsies preferred travelling at night and hiding themselves during the day.

They had already travelled many miles.

Even if by now her disappearance had been noticed, no one would have the least idea where she could have been taken or in which direction.

She knew the Duke's first thought would be that she had run away.

Then she thought that because he was so clever and so astute, he would discover that she had taken nothing with her.

If she was planning to go abroad, as she had suggested, he would know she would not have travelled in a white evening-gown decorated with forget-me-nots.

She would at least have put something sensible on, calculated not to attract attention.

"Let him find me . . . oh . . . God . . . let him . . . find me!" she pleaded.

At that moment she heard the sound of horses' hoofs.

With a leap of her heart she thought that by some miracle it was the Duke.

She got up and went to the door, putting her ear close against it so as to hear what was happening outside.

Then she heard his voice.

There was no mistaking it as he asked sharply and in a tone of authority:

"I wish to speak to the head of this family. Where is he?"

With a little cry of happiness Katrina began to beat on the bolted door, crying out as she did so:

"I am . . . here! I am . . . here! Save . . . me! Please save . . . me!"

The Duke had felt very anxious as Ramon led him through woods and along uncultivated fields.

Sometimes he could see wheel-marks which he thought might be those of a caravan.

However, the going was rough, as there had been no rain for a long time.

It was hard to distinguish anything that was in any way helpful.

He did not slacken his pace, only trusting Ramon to lead him on the right routes.

He determined that if they did not find Katrina before they reached London, he would have every Policeman in the City out looking for her.

The horses were sweating and they were all, the Duke thought, in need of something to drink, when Ramon, who was riding alongside him, pointed ahead.

Through the trees the Duke could see in the distance the round top of a caravan.

He warned himself sternly not to be too elated.

There were quite a number of gypsies about at this time of the year.

The gypsies he could now see might easily be another clan or tribe.

They would have no knowledge of the gypsies who had been at Lynd.

He drew his horse to a standstill.

As he did so he saw by the expression on Ramon's face that incredible though it seemed, they had found what they were seeking.

As he asked for the head of the gypsies, he heard her voice.

He rode up to where the empty shafts of

the caravan were lying on the ground.

Dismounting, he pulled back the iron bolt on the door.

As soon as he did so, Katrina came out.

She stood for a moment on the small platform on which was the driver's seat.

She looked down at him and her eyes were alight with joy.

There was an expression of such radiance on her face that the Duke thought she looked more beautiful than he remembered.

Then, convinced it really was the Duke and she was safe, she gave a little cry.

It was very moving, and she literally threw herself into his arms.

He caught her.

As he held her close against him, she hid her face against his shoulder, saying incoherently:

"You have . . . come! I prayed . . . and prayed that Papa . . . would . . . send you . . . and now . . . you are . . . here!"

"I have found you," the Duke said, "and this shall never, never happen again!"

Then, because she had been so frightened, Katrina burst into tears.

He could feel her whole body shaking as she cried against him.

He knew then that he was overwhelmingly in love as he had never been in love with any woman before.

He had known it, he thought, when he had lain awake trying to puzzle out what had happened to her.

He had known as he planned exactly how he would force Anastasia to tell him the truth.

He had, however, not really admitted it to himself.

Not even when he was straining every nerve in his body as he rode after her, terrified that he might not find her.

Now he knew she was everything he had ever wanted, everything he had thought it impossible to find.

It all flashed through his mind.

As his arms tightened instinctively around her, he could feel her slim body quivering against his own.

He knew then that he would protect her, take care of her, and love her for ever.

Never again would he allow her to be unhappy or afraid.

"It is all right," he said soothingly, stroking her long hair. "I am here, and nothing shall hurt you."

As he spoke, he thought of the bawdy house into which Anastasia had told the gypsies to sell her.

He decided it was something about which she must never know.

At the sound of his voice, Katrina, with what he thought was admirable self-control, forced herself to stop crying.

Then, with his arms still around her, the Duke looked round.

He intended to speak to the gypsies, only to find that they had gone.

There were three caravans and three horses which were searching for grass amongst the undergrowth in the wood.

There was a smouldering fire, and a few utensils with which they had cooked their meal.

But there was not a sign of any human being except themselves.

The Duke then looked at Ramon for explanation.

He came towards him, holding the bridles of both their horses.

As if the Duke had already asked the question, he explained:

"They know they've done wrong, Yer Grace, so they've run off. They'll not come back 'til we've gone."

"The sooner we leave here, the better!" the Duke said.

He looked down at Katrina, who had not raised her head, and said:

"Miss Darley will ride in front of my saddle. Find a blanket for her to sit on and a shawl to prevent her from being cold."

He drew a sovereign from his waistcoat pocket as he spoke and threw it towards Ramon, who caught it deftly.

Leaving the horses, who had no wish to roam, he climbed into the caravan which Katrina had just left.

He brought out a blanket from her bed.

He put it on the Duke's saddle, then went to one of the other caravans.

The doors were open and the interior of each one was a jumble of various articles.

These included wicker-baskets and clothes-pegs which the gypsy women made and sold from house to house when they came to a village.

Ramon picked up a knotted shawl which was not new, but clean, having obviously been recently washed.

He brought it back to the Duke.

It was white and he put it over Katrina's shoulders and as he did so she looked up at him.

"I . . . I did not . . . think you would . . . ever find me," she whispered.

"I would have found you, even if you had been carried away to the moon!" he said. "Now, as we have had enough dramatics, I am going to take you somewhere safe and make sure this sort of thing never happens again."

She looked up at him for explanation and he smiled as he said:

"Leave everything to me."

"That is . . . what I want . . . to do," she murmured with a little choke in her voice.

Her eye-lashes were wet with tears, but her eyes were shining.

The Duke knew he wanted, more than he had ever wanted anything in his life, to kiss her.

But he thought it would be a mistake.

Instead, he picked her up in his arms and set her on Conqueror's back.

Then carefully mounting the horse himself, he put his left arm round her while he held the reins with his right.

As they moved off and Ramon followed them, keeping a short distance behind, Katrina said:

"It is . . . true that you are . . . really here . . . and I am not . . . dreaming?"

"I am really here," the Duke affirmed, "and I want you to forget all that has happened, and instead think only happy thoughts until we reach London."

"London?" Katrina asked. "Are we going to London?"

"It is nearer than Lynd from here," he said, "and I have plans which will make everything easier for us than if we return to Lynd, where we would have to make long explanations, which I am sure you would hate."

Katrina gave a little shiver.

She had thought she would have to face Anastasia, and that would be very embarrassing.

She also thought Aunt Lucy would be angry because she had drawn attention to herself.

Then, because it seemed natural, she put her head against the Duke's shoulder.

She thought that like Perseus he had come to her rescue and she need no longer be afraid.

It did not take them very long to reach the Duke's house in Park Lane.

Although the servants must have been surprised to see them, they were too well-trained to do anything but welcome their master.

The Duke ordered the Housekeeper to take Katrina to one of the main bedrooms.

She went upstairs, not wishing to leave him, but reassured because he had said:

"Rest now, and I will come to talk to you later."

The Housekeeper was too tactful to ask questions.

She made, instead, disapproving noises at the creases in Katrina's expensive gown.

She produced, as if by magic, a very attractive nightgown.

She said it had been left behind by one of the Duke's guests.

"I am afraid I have nothing to wear but what I have on," Katrina said.

Although she saw the curiosity in the Housekeeper's eyes, she did not say any more.

When Katrina was comfortably in bed, some food was brought to her.

She ate it because she was, to her surprise, a little hungry.

She could not help thinking it would have been more exciting to have had luncheon with the Duke.

She was not complaining, however, because it was so wonderful to know that she was here in his lovely house.

That she was safe where no one could hurt her.

"Thank You . . . thank You . . . God!" she said fervently.

She was sure as she prayed that it was her father who had told the Duke how to find her.

It was so lucky that he had a man in his employ who knew the gypsy ways and their secret routes as no ordinary groom would have done.

Her tray was taken away and as time went by she thought that the Duke must have forgotten her.

Then at last the door opened and he came in.

He was looking very smart, and she thought no man could look more exciting or more masculine.

Then she blushed because such an idea had come to her mind.

She expected him to sit on a chair which the Housekeeper had left near her.

Instead, he sat on the bed, and, taking her hand in his, said gently:

"You are all right? They did not hurt you?"

"No . . . but I was . . . so frightened because the gypsy girl who looked after me told me I was to be . . . s-sold when we reached London . . . and I could not . . . understand why . . . anyone would want to . . . buy me."

She felt the Duke's fingers tighten on hers before he said:

"I want you to forget everything that has happened."

"I will try to," Katrina said, "but I was so . . . afraid you would . . . think that I had . . . run away and would not . . . bother to look for me."

"I might possibly have thought that," the Duke agreed, "if I had not learnt you had taken nothing with you but what you were wearing, and that was an evening-gown!"

Katrina gave a little cry of delight.

"I knew . . . you would be . . . clever enough to . . . realise that! But . . . how did . . . you . . . guess that I had been . . . kidnapped?"

"I found some flowers from your hair in the garden, and it seemed very strange that they should have become dislodged, and perhaps roughly."

"You are clever . . . so very . . . very clever!"

Because he realised it had to be said once and for all, the Duke told her how he had learned that Anastasia had stopped to talk to the gypsies on the previous day.

He told her that when he challenged her with having paid them to take her away, she had been forced to admit it.

"She . . . she told you . . . the truth?" Katrina asked in wonder.

The Duke knew that she was too intelligent not to realise that Anastasia would never have told him the truth voluntarily.

"I had to use a little persuasion," he admitted, "but that is something I do not wish to talk about. Instead, I have made a great many plans for us to which I hope you will agree."

"P-plans?"

Now there was a definite expression of anxiety in Katrina's eyes.

As her fingers trembled in his, he knew perceptively that she was thinking he intended to send her away.

She thought that perhaps after all, he was accepting her suggestion that she should go abroad and disappear.

That was why he had brought her to London so that no one would know what had happened.

The Duke looked into her eyes which were very revealing.

Then he said quietly:

"I think, darling, you must be aware by this time that I love you!"

There was silence.

Then Katrina said in a voice that did not sound like her own:

"D-did you say . . . you . . . loved me?"

"I love you!" the Duke confirmed. "And what I have suffered in the last few hours has made me determined that I will never lose you again!"

As he spoke he bent forward.

Almost before Katrina could realise what was happening, his lips were on hers.

As he kissed her, he knew it was the most perfect kiss he had ever known.

He was gentle, and yet Katrina felt there was a fire on his lips.

As the pressure of them deepened and became more possessive, more demanding, she felt the wonder of it move like a light within her body.

Then she knew that this was all she had ever longed for and thought she would never know.

Her lips were soft, sweet, and innocent, yet at the same time the Duke realised she surrendered herself to him.

He put his arms around her and held her so close that it was hard for her to breathe.

His kisses seemed to Katrina to carry her into the sky and the world was forgotten with everything in it which had frightened or upset her.

After a long time the Duke raised his head.

"How can you make me feel like this?" he asked. "I never knew, and this is the truth, my precious, that love could be so wonderful."

"Do you . . . mean that? Do you . . . really mean it?" Katrina exclaimed.

"I swear to you, I know now I have never been in love before."

He knew that was true.

He had loved Anastasia wildly as a young man loves for the first time, but it was purely physical attraction.

The desire of his body for hers, from the burning fire she ignited in him.

What he felt for Katrina was different.

Because she was so young and so unspoiled, she was like a flower that he must treat very gently and never inadvertently bruise or damage.

She was also, and he knew it now, what he had always wanted to find in the wife he would take to Lynd.

She would fill his mother's place, and, at the same time, belong utterly and completely to him.

Suddenly he realised why she was so different from the other women in his life.

It was because she was good.

It was an old-fashioned word, but he acknowledged that compared to Katrina all his so-called loves had been bad women.

What he felt now was true love.

The love he had always sought unconsciously, but which had made him declare he would never marry until, like the Golden Fleece, he found it.

Aloud he said:

"I love you! And I intend to go on saying so until you believe me."

"I . . . I want to believe you," Katrina said. "But when I . . . loved you, I thought you would . . . never love me . . . because I am so . . . insignificant and unimportant . . . beside your other friends."

"You are very different from what you call my 'friends,' " the Duke said, "and what I feel for you, my darling, is a love which we both know, because we have been in the East, is ageless and eternal."

He saw her eyes light up, and he went on:

"I believe we found each other in other lives, and now we have found each other in this. Together we will go on into eternity, because we are complete in each other and can never be parted."

Katrina gave a cry of sheer delight, then she said:

"That is what I want you to feel! But you are so . . . magnificent, that I thought I could . . . never mean . . . anything to . . . you."

"To me you are the moon, the stars and the sun — the whole world!" the Duke said passionately.

Then he was kissing her again.

Kissing her fiercely, as if he not only wanted to make sure she was his, but also to conquer her, so that she would never think of anyone except him.

Only when they were both breathless did he say a little incoherently:

"And now, my darling heart, we must make plans, but when you look at me like that, all I want to do is to kiss you and words are unimportant."

"That is . . . what I want . . . too," Katrina said, "but I want to hear your plans . . . even though I am a . . . little afraid . . . of what they might be."

"There is no need to be," the Duke assured her, "because I think you will want what I want, and that is that we should be married immediately."

"M-married?"

"Your uncle and aunt gloated because they thought they had forced me into a position where I had to marry you," the Duke said.

There was a happy note in his voice, and he continued:

"But while we want to be together, I know you will feel as I do, that we want no one at our marriage except ourselves."

Katrina put her arms around his neck.

"How can you think of . . . anything so . . .

marvellous?" she asked. "Can we really be alone . . . just with . . . God? And I know that Papa and Mama will be . . . there too."

"That is what I thought you would think," the Duke said. "Actually, I had sent someone to London to get a Special Licence for the wedding your aunt was so busily arranging in the Chapel at Lynd. But now we are going to be married in a Church which is only a little way from here."

Katrina drew in her breath.

"Just . . . you and . . . me?"

"Just us!"

She raised her lips to his in a gesture of gratitude, and he kissed her very gently before he said:

"Then, my precious, before anyone can realise what has happened, we are going away. You wanted to run away and hide, and I think that is a good idea, only I intend to come with you, so you will never be alone, or frightened."

There was no need for Katrina to speak.

She looked, the Duke thought, as if a thousand candles had been lit inside her.

There was a radiance in her face which left him speechless.

Then, as if she felt she must be practical, she said:

"I suppose you . . . know I have . . .

nothing to wear except this . . . nightgown which I have . . . borrowed?"

The Duke laughed and it was a very happy sound.

"That is something I have already thought of. In fact, I have sent round to your uncle's house to collect everything you did not take with you to Lynd."

He kissed her forehead and went on:

"I have also arranged for your clothes from Lynd to be sent to us where no one will know, except my secretary, where we will be."

"It sounds very . . . very . . . exciting!" Katrina murmured.

"It will be, I promise you," the Duke answered, "but we are going on a very long honeymoon, my darling."

"Where are we going?"

"To the sort of exciting places you went with your father and mother," the Duke answered, "but this time you will be travelling in comfort."

He looked at her to see if she was excited, then he said:

"I thought to-morrow morning we might leave for Paris, where I can buy you some of the things I expect you will need for your trousseau, and the presents which I long to give you because you will be my wife."

Katrina pressed herself a little closer to him and he went on:

"Then we will pick up my yacht at Marseilles, and I thought it would amuse you to visit Tunisia, which I have not visited before, and I don't think you have either."

Katrina gave him a delighted smile as he continued:

"After that we might go down the Suez Canal. I feel the East calls us both and that is where we can learn so many things which will help and inspire us when we return to our life here."

"Perhaps," Katrina murmured, "I ought . . . not to take . . . you away from your . . . duties. You are . . . after all . . . a very . . . very important . . . person."

"I shall carry out my 'duties,' as you call them, very much better when we return," the Duke said firmly. "You will help and inspire me, my lovely one, and I know stimulate me to be a much better man than I am now, and a better servant to Her Majesty and to our country."

"How could I ever have . . . dreamed or imagined that you would speak to me like that?" Katrina asked. "You know those are the . . . things I want for . . . you."

She pressed her cheek against his shoulder as she went on:

"I am only . . . sorry that I cannot . . . help you to be a . . . King, so that you could rule over people in a country which would be the happiest one there has ever been!"

The Duke laughed.

"We have our own country," he said, "and even if it is not very large, it will be a country of love, and we can help all those who look to us for help to be as happy as we are ourselves."

"I will do . . . everything to make you . . . happy," Katrina said, "but you must . . . help me and teach me and . . . prevent me from . . . making mistakes."

"What could be easier?" the Duke said. "All you have to do is to love me and everything will come out right."

He thought to himself that it was a strange thing for him to say.

Yet it came from the depths of his heart.

He knew that Katrina, with her spiritual perceptiveness and her instinct for what was right and what was wrong, would shine like a star.

He would find himself following her all through his life.

Then, because she was so soft and sweet and utterly adorable, he wanted to think not only of her soul but of her heart.

In a few hours she would be his wife.

He kissed her until the room spun dizzily around them.

He felt a little flame in Katrina respond to the fire burning fiercely within him.

He knew that to teach her the joys and delights of love would be the most exciting thing he had ever done.

With what was a super-human effort he said:

"I must leave you now, my precious wife-to-be. Your clothes will be here soon and I want you to look very beautiful for our wedding."

"You . . . promise you will not be . . . disappointed in me?" Katrina asked.

"That is something I could never be," he said. "You are mine, my darling, mine, and I love you!"

"As I love you!" she whispered. "How can I ever thank God enough for . . . letting us . . . find each other?"

"We have this life, and all eternity in which to do so," the Duke said quietly.